AN UNKNOWN SOLDIER

DAVID JAMES MADDEN

An Unknown Soldier

For information about this title or to order other books and/or electronic media, contact the publisher:
David James Madden
Westerly, RI
www.davidjamesmadden.com
davidjamesmadden67@gmail.com

Library of Congress Control Number: 2019907779

ISBN:
- Hardcover: 978-0-9843119-2-7
- Softcover: 978-0-9843119-3-4
- eBook: 978-0-9843119-4-1

Printed in the United States of America

Chapter illustration by Polly Seip. Polly's work can be seen on Instagram: polly_seip

Cover and Interior design: 1106 Design

To Nick Checker,
for helping me bring *An Unknown Soldier* to life.

"If you bring forth what is within you, what you bring forth will save you. If you do not bring forth what is within you, what you do not bring forth will destroy you."

—JESUS IN THE GOSPEL OF THOMAS

CHAPTER ONE

Men Without Faces

THE FIRST RUMBLE OF thunder was too far away to awaken Peter Franklin, but deep within the secret realm of his unconscious mind, a dream formed in response to the sound. A minute passed, and then a sharp, though still-distant, thunderclap released the dream from unconsciousness. Strange, troubling images ascended to his mind's eye. He tossed over to his left side and then back to his right, but he did not wake up.

In his dream, Peter was no longer seventy-two with a face wrinkled and creased by years in the sun, and thinning gray hair, but strong and young with curly brown hair, a flat stomach, and once-again-supple arms and legs. As strong as he was, however, he could barely keep his head above waves that slapped across his face, making it hard for him to take in a desperately needed breath. There was a large tree jutting up out of the water. In between the waves striking him in the face, Peter caught glimpses of a desolate shore shrouded in acrid smoke. Though the shore was close, he was unable to move toward it. His arms and legs felt as though they were weighed down by iron cables. Treading water frantically, he caught sight of several men without faces standing on the shore. Peter waved and shouted to them. As they noticed him, he saw that they were clutching huge guns in their hands. Suddenly, in unison, the faceless men leveled the guns in Peter's direction and fired. Somehow, he managed to take cover behind the large tree before the bullets could hit their mark.

Peter glanced to his right and saw there was another man in the water, someone in even more danger than him. This man was the same age as Peter, with the same short-cut hair and strong, young body. He had a narrow face barely old enough to be shaved. His frightened pale-blue eyes darted around about him, with all the distress of a little boy separated from his mother on a bustling city street. The man's head bobbed above and beneath the water like a cork at the end of a fishing line. When the man broke the surface, there was a look of helplessness on his face that filled Peter with a terrible sadness. He called out to the terrified man in a voice so choked by sobs that he could barely wrest the words from his throat.

Because of the faceless men with guns, Peter dared not move any closer to the man, though he desperately wanted to help. He gazed toward the shore and saw that more faceless men with guns had gathered there. They, too, started shooting at him and the unknown man. The bullets splashing in the water were like handfuls of sand being thrown by children playing a deadly game.

Peter screamed at the faceless men to stop shooting, but they only laughed maliciously and continued firing all the more. He glanced back at the panicked man and saw him slip under the water as bullets splattered all around him. He surfaced again and caught sight of Peter. His child-like eyes pleaded for help. Peter stared in horror as water began to swirl down the man's open mouth the way it drains out of a sink. His eyes bulging with fear, the man sank beneath the surface of the water while Peter cried out to him over and over again. As if in reply, the man's head bobbed back up. He stared at Peter with an unwavering glare until slowly submerging under the waves for the last time. Peter wept because he had not dared to help the young man with the pale-blue eyes.

A crack of thunder jolted Peter out of his dream. For a moment, in the storm-darkened morning's half-light, he was disoriented. He managed to slip on his glasses just as a sharp burst of lightning illuminated the room. Though Peter recognized his bureau, the nightstand, wall lamp, chairs, and bed, everything now appeared foreign to him. Had he awakened in the bedroom of a total stranger? Or was this room the dream, and the reality the water and the brutal, faceless men trying to kill him and that other man? He couldn't be sure.

Peter's breath caught in his throat, and he sat bolt upright. Beads of sweat covered his forehead and trickled down across his face. He shivered from the chilly wind blowing in upon him through the open window just over his head. He took in a few deep breaths to try to calm himself.

Another brilliant flash lit up the window shades, and a clap of thunder shook the walls. He caught sight of himself in the mirror of the dresser. In that instant, his gray pallor, sunken eyes, and disheveled hair gave him the sensation he was observing his own corpse. The room seemed to shrink in, threatening to crush him.

He sprang out of bed and stood transfixed as his familiar bedroom was turning into a coffin, burying him alive.

Peter flipped on a light and stared at his image to assure himself he wasn't a corpse after all. With trembling fingertips, he touched the stubble on his face, his bushy eyebrows, and his large, protruding ears. He patted his hands over his slender shoulders and rubbed his paunch. Convinced he was still alive, but still shaking violently, he picked up a favorite photograph of his daughter-in-law and granddaughter together in their garden. It was the one he always kept on the nightstand next to his bed. He stared at the picture of Jennifer and Heidi, forcing himself to focus on their smiling faces, each with a daisy woven into their sandy blond hair. He recalled all the laughter he had shared with the two of them the last time they had come to visit him. *When was that, anyway?*

Three years ago? Four? Too long—much too long a time. Such a beautiful child and such a lovely mother. *They're my family. I hope I can see them again soon. Perhaps another visit might be arranged. Yes, that can be done. I will see them again soon. Of course, I will. Perhaps even Richard. Even that is possible.*

Clutching the picture to his heart, he paced back and forth. He fought an impulse to rush outside into the storm to escape the nameless fear squeezing in upon him. He raised a window shade and stared out at as lightning revealed, for a moment, the maple trees in his yard tossing about wildly in the storm. He counted the seconds between a flash of lightning and a peal of thunder.

The intervals lengthened as the storm rolled away. He continued breathing in deeply as anxiety seeped away little by little. Finally, with lightning on the horizon but no longer any sound of thunder, he turned back to his bed. Drenched in sweat, he collapsed upon it.

Peter glanced over at the clock on the nightstand by his bed. It was 6:30 AM on June 6th.

Fifty years to the day, he thought. *My God, to the very minute.*

He forced his eyelids to stay open, afraid he would dream again of cruel, faceless men and the helpless man who died because he had been too afraid to help him. But an hour later, when the clouds parted and sunlight filtered languidly through his curtains, Peter was sound asleep.

CHAPTER TWO
The Night Before

WITH HIS HEAD IN HIS HANDS, Richard Franklin appeared to be intently reading something, but there was nothing on the desk in front of him. His daughter, Heidi, pausing before she entered his study, noticed this. For a moment, she wanted to turn away and go back to her bedroom. Instead, she knocked softly on the door.

Richard looked up. His dark-circled, deep-set eyes stared straight ahead without appearing to see anything. His hair was disheveled, and he hadn't shaved for a few days. He had the confused look of someone who has been asleep and isn't sure where he is when he first wakes up. To Heidi, he looked like one of the people at the homeless shelter she served dinner to once a month with her church youth group. She felt an even stronger urge to flee to her room. But when her father squinted in her direction, she smiled and walked in.

"Hi, Dad," she said with what she hoped sounded like genuine cheerfulness. She sat down in the chair on the other side of the desk. "What are you doing?"

Richard ran his fingers through the graying hair around his temples. His eyes darted about anxiously, as if searching for an answer to Heidi's question. What was a reasonable explanation for sitting alone in a darkening room? On the night before his daughter was leaving for college, no less? Nothing came to him. Trying to sound casual and relaxed, he finally said, "Oh, not too much, actually."

He pulled the chain on his brass lamp. Light radiated out from under the thick, green-glass shade. Heidi was taken aback. The angle of the light accented the lines of anxiety etched across her father's face. He looked gaunt and haggard, older than his forty-four years.

She had resolved, before entering the room, that she was going to confront him. Why wasn't he going to go with her tomorrow when she left for her first semester at Fillmore College? She had rehearsed what she was going to say. She probably wouldn't be back until Thanksgiving. She wanted him to see the campus. To be there with her when she got those butterflies that always appeared when she was doing something for the first time.

Now, as Heidi regarded his sorrowful eyes, she knew he wasn't going to join her tomorrow, no matter what she said. It was just what her mother had told her once when she had gone off to summer camp for a week. For some reason, her father couldn't ever bring himself to say a simple goodbye. It would do no good to try to convince him otherwise. She might get angry if she attempted to persuade him. She might even cry. Then she'd feel bad the next day about making him worry about her. She willed herself to let it go. Her father was who he was.

Heidi raised herself lithely to curl her long, willowy legs up on the chair, as if she planned to sit with him for a while. He smiled hesitantly and felt relieved to see her smile back at him.

"I bought some new shoes today," she said nonchalantly as she gathered two strands of her long hair, sun-bleached by her summer as a lifeguard at Crystal Lake. With the strands only a few inches from her tanned face, each accented the other. As she sat, absorbed in coiling her hair into a braid, Richard thought his daughter had the looks to be on the cover of a Beach Boys album.

Richard recalled how Jennifer used to often braid Heidi's hair when she was a little girl. He wanted to mention this but instead said nothing. She peered up at him.

"What did you get?" he said when he noticed her puzzled expression over his lack of a response.

She went back to focusing on her hair.

"Running shoes?"

"Yeah, they were on sale, so I just decided to get them."

"That's good. I'm glad you did that," said Richard. Heidi frowned at the listless tone in his voice.

She let go of her half-braided hair and scanned the room. Her eyes went to her father's immaculately preserved fire trucks, his Christmas gifts from years ago. The pumper when he was in second grade, the hook and ladder in third. The plastic box containing his childhood View-Master reels. The twelve-book series of *The Golden Book History of the United States.* He had told her once how he had collected the books one volume at a time, using his paper-route money and going to the A&P every two weeks for the latest in the series. The plastic model of a baseball player swinging a bat, a souvenir of Yankee Stadium. Nothing gave her an idea for beginning a conversation.

"It'll be so weird not running cross-country this year," she said just above a whisper. "I wouldn't have had time for it, though. Not with the course load I have this semester. But I can still run on my own."

Aware that he had come across as uninterested a moment ago, Richard nodded vigorously to show he was now being attentive.

"It's a very pretty campus," she said. "It'll be nice to run there. Lots of trails. Very pretty. You would . . ." She felt anger rising up in her throat and stopped herself.

"I called Grandpa Pete a little while ago," she continued after waiting a few seconds to be sure her emotions were now under control.

"Oh, that's good." Richard's voice remained flat.

Heidi hesitated.

"He wished me good luck and then said I wouldn't need it." Why was she talking about her grandfather? Was she trying to upset *him* to get even for upsetting *her*? She watched him needlessly straighten a small pile of papers on the side of his desk.

"You're busy; I should go," she said but didn't make a move to get up. Thoughts swirled through her mind: *What's wrong with you, Heidi? Just say 'Good night' already. What are you trying to prove? Leave now before you say something you'll regret later.*

"No, that's okay," he said and quickly put the papers down. The last thing he wanted was for his daughter to leave the room.

For a moment, instead of a young woman about to begin college, Richard saw the little girl in pigtails Heidi had once been. The image was so vivid that he shut his eyes and shook his head to dismiss it.

With his eyes still shut tight, a thought flashed through his mind. What he wanted was for this little girl he saw in his mind's eye to kiss him good night and then go to her room, because tomorrow would be her first day of second grade . . . first grade . . . kindergarten. He wanted to walk with her down the street the next day. Wait with her until Mr. Ellis, the skinny crossing guard with the beaming smile, signaled to them. He wanted to take her hand in his and cross the street to Woodbury Elementary School.

But did you ever do that with her, Richard? Even once? No!
You were never there to see her off for a first day of school.

That always fell to Jennifer. He always said that he had to be early at the high school. He wanted to be ready, so he claimed, for his first class on the first day. That was the excuse he gave every year. What was his excuse now?

Richard opened his eyes, wondering who he would see: a young woman about to leave home for college or a pigtailed little girl waiting for her good-night kiss. His daughter was staring at him, directly, steadily, intensely. He felt tears threaten to well up in his eyes. Afraid he might break down and cry if he met her gaze, he studied his hands.

"I guess I'd better get to bed," said Heidi through a lump in her throat. She rose from the chair. "We—that is, Mom and I—have an early start tomorrow."

"Wait a second," said Richard.

She turned quickly to him, her eyes suddenly wide with hope.

He had no idea what to say.

She saw this at once. The burst of anticipation drained from her face.

Unable to bear seeing her disappointment, he bolted from his chair, drew near to her, and hugged her tight.

After a few moments, she pushed away from him firmly yet gently.

He saw the questions in her eyes but couldn't bring himself to respond to her.

I know what you want to ask, Heidi. What's wrong with me? What makes me act this way? I would tell you if I could, but I don't know. I just don't know.

He caught a glimpse of her mother in Heidi's gaze. More than once in the past twenty-one years, he had wondered how it could be that Jennifer had married him. Now he wondered how this beautiful, strong, confident young woman could be his daughter. Jennifer's daughter also, of course. There was so much of her mother in her. But him? How could that be?

"Heidi, I'm sorry—"

She broke away from him before he could finish. He was surprised how easily she was able to free herself from him.

An athlete, like her mother.

She strode out of the room without another word. He stood where he was, hoping she might walk back into the room. Tell him not to worry. Say she understood. Assure him it was alright that he wouldn't be coming with her the next day. Let him know it was okay that only her mother, as always, would take her to school tomorrow.

Richard heard the door to her room down the hall slam shut. It became quiet enough to hear the ticking of the clock on the wall behind him, each rhythmic beat adding to the sadness weighing him down. He felt overwhelmed by a sorrow so thick and heavy he feared he would collapse if he didn't sit down at once. Stumbling his way to his chair, he turned off the light from the brass lamp and, in the darkness, rested his head in his hands once more.

CHAPTER THREE

They Double the Fines This Weekend

THE NEXT MORNING, Richard hurried out of the house right after breakfast. When Jennifer realized he had left, she told herself she didn't care where he was going or when he was coming back. She tried driving his absence out of her mind, but this only made her think about it all the more. She tried to convince herself she wasn't upset, but, as with all her attempts at subterfuge when it came to Richard, she was not successful.

The stress of dealing with her husband's latest disappearing act, this time on the day their daughter was leaving for college, had drained Jennifer's already depleted energy. She felt enveloped by an invisible weight pushing against her from all directions. She strained against every effort she made: making the bed, carrying the laundry basket down to the basement, emptying the dishwasher. She felt like she was in an old dream where she was running as fast as she could but remaining stuck in place.

To make matters worse, Heidi was not her normal, easygoing, good-natured self. Jennifer, recognizing the signs of a restless night's sleep, held her tongue as her daughter uncharacteristically fussed over every wrinkled shirt, missing CD, and broken shoe-lace. The lighthearted banter they usually shared was replaced by a disconcerting silence. As the minutes went by, Jennifer's anxiety and fatigue fed off each other. She went from room to room with a growing sensation of being an intruder in someone else's home.

Pausing for a moment to force a smile, she entered Heidi's room to help her pack. When Heidi acted like she wasn't even there, it was more than Jennifer could handle. She bolted back to her own bedroom and shut the door tight behind her. Overwhelmed, she wanted to throw herself on her bed and cry into her pillow.

Instead, Jennifer sat on the edge of the bed and gazed out the window. She listened to the music of field crickets and katydids as the soft, mellow light of late summer shimmered on the dry, brown grass. The mid-morning air was warming rapidly. Some of the leaves bordering the backyard were already starting to turn. From one of the trees came the continuous, high-pitched buzzing sound of a cicada. The whine grew louder and louder for several seconds and then stopped abruptly. As Jennifer observed summer and autumn intermingling, she felt the same bittersweet ache she always experienced at this time of year. What was it she longed for when summer began fading away? As always, she didn't know.

All Jennifer did know was that nothing about this day was turning out how she'd imagined it would. After a few minutes, feeling somewhat more composed, she got up from the bed and went back to Heidi's room. She saw there wasn't much left to do now but bring the suitcases, boxes, and bins out to the car. She was relieved to see that Heidi had done almost everything by herself. But this display of her child's adult-like independence also brought on another wave of melancholy. Rather than continue to succumb to these feelings, she forced herself to pick up a suitcase and carry it outside.

When the car was finally packed with everything Heidi was taking, Jennifer turned the ignition key and backed slowly out of the driveway. As they drove off, she realized she could hardly remember a thing about the day from the moment she had awakened. This worried her. *Am I starting to lose my mind? Could too much stress really do that?*

Before they'd even reached the highway, Heidi had curled herself up into a ball and closed her eyes. It bothered Jennifer that Heidi was sitting with her back to her. She resisted the temptation to give Heidi a little nudge to see if she was really sleeping. Was her daughter actually ignoring her by pretending to sleep?

Jennifer told herself to hush. *Keep your eyes on the road. Set the cruise control. Now, just drive.*

She normally enjoyed driving. But even with the light traffic and the good weather, her neck and shoulders felt tight. She seethed when a car got too close to her rear bumper, something she usually didn't even notice. "Good Vibrations" started playing on the oldies radio station she always kept the car radio tuned to. She went to turn up the volume a little but then decided not to, in case Heidi was actually sleeping. Even with the sound turned down low, the Beach Boys, as they always did, brightened her mood. She realized she had been squeezing the steering wheel so tightly that her hands were beginning to ache. She relaxed her grip and felt her shoulders loosening up.

After several miles had passed, Jennifer found herself wishing she had written down all the things she had daydreamed of saying to Heidi over the past year. Some nights, while she was lying in bed, just before she fell asleep, the words had come to her in a steady stream of perfectly structured sentences. Now, except for scattered words here and there, Jennifer's mind was a blank.

Why hadn't I just once in the past twelve months jumped out of bed and run into Heidi's room? Why hadn't I shaken her awake so I could share all my wise thoughts on love and sex, on drinking and drugs? She stopped herself and smiled wryly at the thought. Heidi would have thought she had gone crazy if she had done that! *But at least I'd have expressed—that one time—what I want to share.* Now of all the profound thoughts she had grown weepy over during the past year when sleep had been only minutes away, the only one that came to mind was *You're everything to me.*

She unconsciously gripped the steering wheel tightly again. It would be better to say nothing than to utter something so inane. So trite. She grew annoyed with herself. Her neck began to ache again.

Jennifer tried to distract herself. What might have been happening on this day one year ago? Most likely, Heidi would have been at the high school, getting ready for her senior year of cross-country. How short that final season had been. How short her whole senior year had been! It seemed to Jennifer now that Heidi had been a high school freshman only a year ago. Was it really possible she was now heading off for her freshman year of college?

Lost in such thoughts, Jennifer was startled when Heidi suddenly inhaled a sharp little snore. She had been sleeping after all! *Good, that's so much better than ignoring me.* Jennifer glanced over to the passenger seat. Heidi's sleepy eyes darted around as she attempted to orient herself. Once she recognized where she was, she looked over at her mother, beamed a goofy, still half-asleep smile, and said, "Hi, Momma."

Is the sullen imposter who had been impersonating Heidi gone? Has my delightful daughter returned to me after napping for less than half an hour?

Jennifer winked at Heidi without taking her eyes off the road. Her mind was racing. Fillmore College was drawing closer with every passing mile. If she was going to say something insightful and prudent, now was the time. Her grip on the steering wheel tightened even more. It was now or never. What could she say?

For God's sake, don't get too heavy. But nothing frivolous, either. Don't make it sound rehearsed. But don't come across as just winging it, either. Where have all my fine words over the past year gone? It's always been so easy to talk with her. Why can't I get a word out now?"

Another mile rolled by. She peeked over at Heidi again and let slip, "Did you get a chance to talk to your father this morning before you left?"

What the hell! Did I actually just say that—of all things? What kind of mother would make such an asinine comment? She snuck another glance just as Heidi squinted and murmured, "Yeah."

Jennifer knew, without a doubt, that she was hopelessly inadequate as a parent, an utter failure as a mother. She again searched her mind for something to say. Not for words of wisdom this time. That was obviously beyond her. Rather, just for something, anything, to make her daughter happy. All Jennifer wanted was for Heidi to be happy. Nothing else mattered.

Just as Jennifer had decided she had no other choice but to keep her mouth shut for everyone's good, Heidi yawned and turned to her.

"I called Grandpa Pete last night," she said.

Relieved that Heidi had unknowingly thrown her a rescue line, Jennifer responded too eagerly. "Did you really?"

Startled by her mother's unexpected burst of intensity, Heidi gaped at her, wide-eyed. Jennifer tried to recover by affecting an air of nonchalance. "What did you talk about?" she asked calmly.

Heidi stared at her dubiously for a moment, looked out the window, and replied, "Not much. He said he wished that he were going off to college, too. I laughed a little when he said that—not to make fun but just to laugh, you know? He told me to make the best of the years ahead. I said I would, and he said he knew I would."

They took an exit off the highway and got on a two-lane country road. Going past a large cornfield on either side of the road, they commented on the height of the stalks. It felt to both of them like they were driving through a jungle.

"I miss Grandpa Pete," mumbled Heidi.

"I know. I miss him, too."

Jennifer wanted to say more about Grandpa Pete, but just then Heidi reached out quickly to search for a different radio station. She stopped when she heard Nirvana playing "Smells Like Teen Spirit." After laughing at each other's musical tastes, they found a soft-rock station they could each tolerate. Jennifer wondered if Heidi had changed the station to distract herself from feeling sad about not seeing her grandfather for such a long time. She decided not to make the mistake of saying anything more about it. *One goof-up is enough for this ride.*

After ten or so more miles had gone by, America's "Sister Golden Hair" lulled Heidi back asleep. When she heard her daughter snoring, Jennifer turned the radio off and mulled over what life with Richard was going to be like from now on.

"How am I ever going to cope without my daughter around?" she asked under her breath. Her eyes darted to Heidi. *God, I hope she didn't hear that!* She was relieved to still hear Heidi's gentle snoring. Attempting to dismiss such thoughts from her mind, Jennifer turned the radio back on and immediately woke Heidi back up.

When a traffic sign told them they were just a few miles away from Fillmore College, Jennifer spontaneously reached over to give her daughter's hand a squeeze. Heidi squeezed her mother's hand back, and neither one of them let go until the school's soccer field came into sight. Jennifer glanced at the field and saw a women's team practicing. *I would have been a good soccer player. I was pretty damn fast in my day.*

They drove between two imposing Ionic columns guarding Fillmore College's entrance and up a slight hill toward the campus. Just past the entrance, a profusion of lavender, pink, burgundy, and bronze chrysanthemums had been planted along each side of the narrow road.

On the spur of the moment, Jennifer stopped the car in the middle of the road to gaze at them.

"Grandpa Pete would love these," said Heidi, thoughts of him fresh in her mind.

"You remembered!" exclaimed Jennifer. "He had all those mums in his garden when we visited him last time, didn't he?"

"I wonder if he still has a garden," mused Heidi, nodding in agreement.

"Maybe, but it wouldn't be as big as the one we saw where your father grew up."

"Right. He couldn't have a big garden at his condo."

Heidi and I haven't seen him since he moved? Is that possible? How long has it been since then? More than three years ago? It couldn't be that long! Could it?

A car horn beeped. Jennifer looked in the rearview mirror to see that four cars had backed up behind them. She shifted back into drive, and they drove up the hill past the flowers.

"My dorm is just past the chapel up ahead," said Heidi.

Jennifer drove past the chapel and kept going past Kearney Hall, Heidi's dorm.

"Momma, the dorm is back there! You just went past it!" Heidi cried out in dismay.

"I know that," answered Jennifer, her palms slippery with sweat on the steering wheel. She turned up the air conditioner. "You could see as well as I could that there wasn't a single parking space."

They drove around in circles several times, driving by Kearney Hall with each pass. Jennifer gritted her teeth each time Heidi let out a high-pitched squeak of exasperation as they drove past the dorm. They sighed with relief in unison when they finally found a place to park, even though Kearney Hall's roofline was far off in the distance. As they were getting out of the car, a pony-tailed young woman with a beaming smile approached them.

"I'm sorry to tell you this, but you really shouldn't park there," she said pleasantly as she pointed to a prominent sign stating in bold, emphatic letters: ABSOLUTELY NO PARKING HERE. The girl shrugged apologetically. "The campus police are pretty strict about parking. They double the fines this weekend," she said with the same glowing smile, much to Jennifer's annoyance.

Jennifer tried to subdue her exasperation. She summoned all her will to force herself to smile back at the girl. "You'd think they'd make it easier to park your car," she muttered through clenched teeth. She could hear how irritated she sounded. The girl raised her eyebrows, raised her hands, and tilted her head in a wordless "Sorry." She continued on her way without a care in the world. Or so it seemed to Jennifer.

They got back into the car and once again drove around in circles searching for a place to park. They finally came upon a charcoal-colored Oldsmobile 88 with rusted-out rocker panels, its backup lights on. It was pulling out of a parking space. Once again, they sighed in unison. Jennifer pushed the turn signal lever up to indicate she was making a right-hand turn.

But the gigantic Olds didn't budge. It stayed right where it was, thick white smoke billowing out of its exhaust pipe. Even with their air conditioner on and the windows raised, fumes from the burning oil of a damaged engine seeped into their car. Cars began to back up behind them. Heidi turned around to see the steadily growing line. "Maybe we'd better try someplace else," she fretted.

"I'm staying here until hell freezes over," replied Jennifer through teeth gritted so tight her jaw ached.

The car finally backed up and drove off in a blinding cloud of smoke. Jennifer slowly and carefully angled their car into the space. In spite of her best efforts, she had to pull out and try again when she didn't get close enough to the curb. Only when she turned the car off did she realize that now Kearney Hall wasn't even in sight. An image of Richard obliviously taking a nap at this moment came to her. Jennifer shook her head to clear the vision out of her mind.

Just as they were getting out of the car, a lean, angular young man approached them. He slowed down to glance at Heidi as she reached into the car's trunk for a suitcase. He did a double take and abruptly came to a stop.

"Heidi?" he asked. "Heidi Franklin?"

When she heard her name, Heidi turned around toward the young man and smiled broadly.

"Hi, Everett," she said. They gave each other a quick loose hug around the shoulders.

"Mom," said Heidi, "this is Everett Dawson. We were on the high school cross-country team together the year before last. Everett, this is my mom."

Everett reached out to shake Jennifer's hand. She noticed Everett wasn't particularly good-looking, but there was a certain air of confidence about him that she immediately liked.

"I didn't know you had decided on Fillmore," said Everett to Heidi. "We should have a good team this year. Are you going to try out?"

Jennifer had worried about her shy daughter being away from home. She felt her spirits lifting as the two young people talked. Maybe this was going to work out after all!

Everett insisted on helping them carry Heidi's stuff to Kearney Hall. He took a shortcut by going around the chapel. Jennifer felt energized by the young man's presence. Several times, she wondered aloud how they would have gotten Heidi's things to her dorm without his help. When she started to say this yet again, a look from Heidi stopped her in mid-sentence. She covered her mouth to hide a sheepish grin.

In her improved mood, Jennifer found herself appreciating Kearney Hall, an imposing, three-story, gothic-style dormitory. Its granite walls, covered in ivy, made her think of a medieval English castle, like the ones she had read about. Students and their parents were carrying suitcases, chairs, lamps, overflowing plastic crates, and armfuls of blankets and pillows through a wide arched doorway. *This will be a good, safe place for Heidi to live while she's away from home—oh, God! Away from me!*

"Thank you so much for your help, Everett," said Jennifer as the three of them stood in Heidi's room after everything had been brought up to the third floor. Heidi repeated her mother's thanks, and, for a couple of seconds, an awkward silence settled over the room. Jennifer wondered if she should leave the room. But where would she go? She couldn't head back for home and leave Heidi with all this work to do. Should she stand in the hall? That would look pretty stupid. Not knowing what to do, she remained fixed in place, her cheeks reddening, in the middle of the room.

"Well, I guess I'll be on my way," said Everett. They both thanked him again, a glance from Heidi telling Jennifer her thanks were a bit too effusive. He turned to leave but stopped at the door. He went to say something but, instead, lowered his eyes, waved goodbye, and left. *He's shy, too, just like Heidi. He's a good guy.*

As soon as Everett left, Jennifer felt energy escaping her body like air out of a balloon that had just been untied. She surveyed the disorganized, jumbled-up mess they had brought into the room. Heidi's roommate had already settled in, and the room had been neat and tidy when they had first walked in. Jennifer knew, from the distant memory of her own not-so-happy experience, just how important a good relationship with a roommate was. She desperately wanted Heidi to make a good first impression. That meant getting the room looking presentable again before the roommate returned. She suddenly felt nauseous and recognized this as a sign of hunger. *Why didn't I bring granola bars? How could I forget?*

"So! Where should we start?" asked Jennifer, forcing herself to sound cheerful. Heidi, sitting on the edge of her unmade bed, just shrugged, her face an expressionless mask. Jennifer felt a prickle of fear. She wished that Everett hadn't left.

"Let's make your bed, shall we?" offered Jennifer tentatively. Heidi got up from the bed but stood like a statue in the middle of the room. Willing herself not to get upset, Jennifer opened first one, then another suitcase, looking for the sheets, pillowcases, blanket, and bedspread. They were nowhere to be found. Jennifer felt panic seeping into her body. She started to ask Heidi where they were but then thought better of it. She happened to glance at a large beach bag that usually held their towels. With yet another sigh of relief, she remembered that was where she had packed the bedding.

As they worked on the room, Jennifer kept alert for just the right moment to share some of her little nuggets of "wisdom." It occurred to her that she had been storing them up like the seashells she had once collected as a child. But every time she thought the moment had arrived, something happened. Two bottles of conditioner but no shampoo. The wrong color for the curtains that had been perfectly fine last week. Then Heidi knocked over the vase containing the peace lily on the windowsill and started to cry. They searched for paper towels to dry the water off the floor as well as Heidi's tears. Finding none, they used the new bath towels.

They still had more to do when a young woman appeared at the door. Jennifer felt a pang: *This must be the roommate!* She introduced herself with her first name only: Jill. Jill then asked Heidi if she had been to the gym yet to get all the "forms and stuff" she needed. Heidi smiled and told her they were on their way, and Jill left with a wave of her hand. Heidi's confident smile immediately dissolved into an expression of panic.

"Mom!" she said, her voice a barely contained shriek. "I have to get to the gym! Right now!"

"But we're almost finished," protested Jennifer. "I'm sure the gym will be open all afternoon."

"Mom! Right now!" commanded Heidi, and Jennifer followed along behind her, running to catch up.

The freshly varnished gym floor shone like a mirror under the bright fluorescent lights. Three large fans made only the slightest dent in the oppressive atmosphere. The heat and humidity of the air outside seemed cool by contrast. Lines of students, some accompanied by parents, stretched away from the tables arranged along the far side of the gym. The walls were covered with posters describing the different clubs and activities offered during the upcoming semester.

Heidi found the line she belonged in and joined it. It appeared to Jennifer to be the longest line. *Of course! What else?* thought Jennifer as she blew a strand of hair off her face. Feeling her calf muscles and lower back going into a spasm, Jennifer tried to stretch her legs without making what Heidi would undoubtedly consider a spectacle of herself. In doing so, she became aware of how much energy there was in the room. Excited, anxious voices were murmuring all around her. An occasional loud laugh or shout pierced the underlying buzz.

Heidi excitedly waved her arm to someone across the gym. Jennifer looked in that direction and saw Everett standing in an open doorway, a wide smile on his face, waving back to Heidi. When he noticed Jennifer, he waved to her politely, but with noticeably less enthusiasm. After a second, Heidi turned back to her mother. Jennifer sensed what was coming next before her daughter even opened her mouth.

"I can take care of my room, Momma."

Her eyes widening, Jennifer swallowed hard. Just like that, the moment had come. Images of Heidi flashed through her mind all at once: delivery room, kindergarten, summer camp, first dance, graduations, birthdays, Christmas mornings . . . and now, right in the middle of a bright, crowded, noisy college gym, this moment of parting, the beginning of a chapter unlike any that had preceded it.

"Well, then, I guess I'll be heading home," said Jennifer, the lump in her throat so huge it seemed to be suffocating her.

"I'll be okay, Momma," said Heidi as she reached out and gave her mother an all-too-brief hug.

"I know you will," said Jennifer. "You'll be swell; you'll be great."

Heidi gently released her mother from her embrace and, holding her firmly by her shoulders, peered into her eyes. "I love you bunches, Momma," she said. When Jennifer gave her their familiar old reply, "I love you bunches back," Heidi smiled. Jennifer let go, turned around, and walked away, forcing herself not to look back.

Jennifer was to the gym's two wide doors when she heard her name being called. She turned around and saw Heidi, her eyes brimming with tears, all but running toward her. Hardly breaking her stride, Heidi collided into her with such force that Jennifer had to take a step back to keep her balance. They embraced tightly, almost as close together as all those years ago, when Heidi had been a baby inside her womb. When they moved apart, they touched foreheads, gazing into each other's eyes. Then Jennifer let her daughter go. Heidi returned to her place in line without either of them having said a word.

Jennifer hadn't noticed the dark clouds that had been gathering when they were walking to the gym. But now, walking back alone to her car, she felt a cold drop of rain on her arm. The first was followed by a second, a third, and then suddenly the sky opened and soaked her before she could unlock the car door.

She sat in silence as rain lashed furiously at the windshield. Without any warning, she first whimpered and then sobbed aloud as the rain pounded furiously on the car.

After about ten minutes, the rain began to let up. Jennifer stopped crying but continued to sit without starting the car. Her tears had finally released a myriad of emotions she had been holding in check for the last couple of weeks. Now an unexpected surge of weariness made her realize how much energy this self-restraint had taken from her.

She closed her eyes and tried to gather herself. After a minute, she contemplated the clearing sky.

Richard should have been with us today. He should have been here with his daughter. With me.

She sat with her thoughts for another minute as the sky continued to brighten.

Face it, Jennifer. Heidi may come home for holidays and vacations, but it will never be the same as it was before today. From now on, it's going to be pretty much just you and Richard.

She jammed the key into the ignition and started the car, ran the wipers a few times, and slowly pulled out of the parking lot. When Jennifer approached the chrysanthemums near the entrance, she checked the rearview mirror and saw there were no cars behind her. She pulled over to the side of the road and considered the mums, now colored even more vividly in the sunlight after the rain.

Heidi was right—Grandpa Pete would love these. Has it really been three years since we saw him last?

She realized with an abrupt, painful jolt that she hadn't invited Peter to Heidi's high school graduation in June. Her eyes filled again with tears.

Oh, God! How could I not have invited Grandpa Pete? It never occurred to me! How is that possible?

She took a slow deep breath and exhaled.

You're right, Jennifer. It never will be the same as it was before today. There are going to be other changes, too. Richard won't be calling all the shots from here on.

She wiped away her tears, put the car in drive, and began the long trip back home, alone.

CHAPTER FOUR

An Assortment of
Washers

All THAT WAS LEFT of the spectacular sunset that followed the brief-but-intense storm was a lingering glow. As he had the night before, Richard sat alone at his desk, only the faintest light in the west-facing window illuminating the room. He was vaguely aware that his mood matched his surroundings.

Jennifer would be back any minute from taking Heidi to Fillmore College. His stomach churned from the worry of her not yet being safely home. Visions of everything from a flat tire to a head-on collision increased his anxiety with each passing minute.

But at the same time, he dreaded whatever the rest of the evening held for him. Would she still be upset he hadn't been there to take Heidi to school? *Probably.* Would she now be angry and ill-tempered or sullen and distant? *Either response would be fully justified.*

Finally, a car turned into the driveway. He leapt to his feet, bumping his leg against the underside of the desk. Cursing, he pulled back the curtain and peeked out the side of the window. He ducked back as headlights momentarily filled the room with a bright, colorless light. As the garage door opened, he felt a surge of relief coursing through his body.

Just as quickly, he felt overcome with self-doubt and shame. He had long suspected he was a failure as a husband. As of today, that also went for being a father.

He turned away from the window. As he did, he caught a glimpse of the full moon out of the corner of his eye. Close to the horizon, it was the color of a pumpkin and appeared much larger than usual. As he gazed at it, he recalled the first time he had seen the moon rising over Big Moose Lake. Memories of long-ago days at the little cottage came to him.

For both Richard and Jennifer, it had been love at first sight of the cottage and its sweeping view of the lake. Jerry Colville, the man who sold them the cottage, had lost his wife, Sally, about a year before and had decided he couldn't live there alone. Jerry had told them after the closing that he saw something of himself and Sally in the young newlyweds, and, so, he wanted them to own the property. For that reason, unbeknownst to them until they attended his funeral years later, he had asked for significantly less than he could have gotten.

Jerry had worked hard at turning the cottage from a summer home to a year-round residence. The electrical and plumbing were up to code, and the galvanized metal roof was good for at least 50 years. Progress on the deck, halted by Sally's death, was nearly half completed. Most of the remaining work was cosmetic and would be fairly simple for an average handyman. But even when Jennifer's parents offered them an interest-free loan, Richard still hadn't been sure that buying the cottage was the right thing to do.

After long talks lasting far into several nights, they finally agreed to go ahead with the purchase. As was his way, Richard kept his feelings of uneasiness hidden from Jennifer right up to the day they signed the papers making them the new owners.

That first evening in their new cottage, they sat on lawn chairs and watched the sunset over the lake. Jennifer noticed how quiet Richard was. She asked him if he was happy.

"Of course, I am," he replied.

"You don't look it. Or sound it, either."

"I'm fine," he answered in an unconvincing tone, but Jennifer didn't press him.

They listened to the chirping of the crickets. A breeze swept in from across the lake, and the leaves around them gently rustled. Then the breeze died down. It became so quiet they could hear the faint call of an owl from somewhere near the lake.

"I'm not even sure which end of the hammer to use when pounding a nail," Richard whimpered.

Jennifer stared at him for a moment, not sure if he were joking, and then she burst out laughing. He folded his arms protectively across his chest. He had been serious. She had misjudged his tone of voice.

"Oh, sweetie," she said, giving his shoulder a squeeze. "I'm sorry. I'm not laughing at you. I thought you were joking around. That was a funny thing to say—and the way you said it."

She held her breath so she wouldn't laugh again, but a guffaw escaped as a snort through her nose. He tried to keep a straight face, but then he laughed, too. Just a little.

"I don't know the first thing about how to build and fix stuff. And now we own this cottage that needs all kinds of work. What in the hell have I gotten myself into?"

Jennifer didn't respond. Instead, she took his hand in hers. Together, they listened to the hooting of the owl harmonizing with the katydids in the mid-August evening. After a minute, she turned to him and said, "I'll be with you every step of the way. We can do this."

She spoke with the confidence he had learned to depend on in the months since they had been married. His bride had a way of making him feel he could do more in life than he had ever believed possible. He wanted then and there to tell her he loved her for that, among many other things. But he kept this thought to himself.

The next day, she gave him a rectangular-shaped package covered in polka-dotted wrapping paper. For a moment, he thought he had forgotten his own birthday. When he tore the paper off, he saw she had bought him a copy of *The Reader's Digest Complete Do-It-Yourself Manual*. On the inside cover, she had written, "We can do anything when we do it together. Love, Jen."

Armed with his manual and tools borrowed from his father-in-law, Richard decided to start off doing small jobs he felt he could handle. On a bright, crisp Saturday morning in mid-September, he undertook his first project: spraying WD-40 on the squeaky hinges of the bedroom door. He swung the door back and forth a few times. The squeak was gone!

He felt a little embarrassed when he turned around to see Jennifer beaming at him. "It's not like I built a new door," he protested as she wrapped her arms around his shoulders and kissed him. Still, he couldn't suppress a little grin. He had begun, and he had been successful.

Armed with a newfound sense of confidence, he announced impetuously that his next job would be to fix the leaky kitchen faucet. Too excited to notice Jennifer's puzzled expression, he got into the car and hurried off.

However, as he drove the twenty minutes to the hardware store, he had second thoughts. He had no idea exactly why the faucet was leaking or what he needed to fix it. By the time he reached the store, he regretted acting so impulsively. He considered going back and talking this over with Jennifer. No, he wanted to show her he could do this. Deep down, he wanted to show himself even more.

When Richard had been a little boy, he had often gone to the neighborhood hardware store with his grandfather. Now, as he entered this hardware store, the varied scents of varnish, wood, rubber, and machine oil greeted him. Memories of his grandfather came rushing back to him. His eyes moistened, and he rubbed them with the back of his hand. He wished his grandfather were with him. He would know immediately what to get. Richard studied the signs at the beginning of each aisle. He found the one marked "Plumbing" and walked to it.

Halfway down the aisle, there was a section devoted to faucets of all kinds: ball, disc, single-handle cartridge, double-handle cartridge, compression. Richard stood wide-eyed before this array. Who was he trying to kid? He had never been handy, and he never would be. Now, standing helpless as a child in the plumbing aisle, he wanted to turn around, go back to the cottage, lock it up, put it on the market, sell it, and never see it again as long as he lived.

"Can I help you, sir?" a reedy voice behind him asked. Richard turned to see a tall, slim, white-haired man with kindly eyes peering at him over reading spectacles that John Adams might have worn. He was wearing a red apron with the store's name *Mackenzie's Hardware* sewn on it in yellow cursive letters. Below the store's name, also in yellow cursive writing, was the man's name: Ernie. He had a pencil, sharpened with a knife, stuck behind his ear.

"I have a leaky faucet," Richard said. Had he actually said that, or had a stranger spoken those words? His neck and face flushed with embarrassment.

Ernie nodded thoughtfully, as if Richard had said something of great significance. "Well, I think we can help you with that." He regarded Richard with a genial expression and, rubbing his hand slowly across his chin, asked him, "What kind of a faucet do you have?"

Richard's mind went blank. He had no idea what kind of faucet he had. He not only couldn't remember what the faucet looked like, he couldn't remember what the kitchen looked like. He couldn't even remember what the cottage looked like. He could only stare forlornly at this friendly older man awaiting an answer.

"Chances are you have a compression faucet. That's the most common type," said Ernie as he pointed to faucets arranged on the top row. Richard grabbed the plastic-encased compression faucet closest to him, thanked Ernie, and started toward the cash registers at the front of the store.

"I was about to say all you might actually need is a washer," called Ernie as Richard hurried away. "I really doubt you need a whole new assembly."

"I've got what I need," said Richard over his shoulder. "Thanks again for your help."

Driving back to the cottage, Richard knew he had made a mistake. The faucet he had grabbed was far more expensive than anything he had expected to pay. As he drove onto the cottage's gravel driveway, he had to face the painful fact that he hadn't a clue as to how to install it. After sitting in the car for a minute, staring into the woods, he finally trudged into the kitchen. Jennifer was sitting at the kitchen table, studying the fix-it-yourself manual she had bought for him.

He sat down beside her. She recognized his lopsided grin as a sign he was embarrassed. He hesitantly pulled the faucet out of the paper bag and placed it before her. Jennifer stared at the faucet, up at him, and then back at the faucet again. A grin curled slowly over her mouth. Richard looked down and braced himself for another one of her outrageous laughs. Instead, he felt her hand curl over his, and when he raised his head, he saw her smiling gently at him. Once again, he found himself falling in love with her. But once again, he didn't tell her.

"You know," she said, her voice just above a whisper, "from what I've been reading, I think all we might need to fix that faucet is a new washer."

"That's what the guy at the hardware store said."

"So why," she asked, choosing her words carefully, "did you decide to buy a whole new faucet?"

"I don't know," he shrugged. "I guess I panicked. All I know is we're stuck with a faucet we don't even need."

"It can be returned."

"I've had enough embarrassment for one day, thank you."

"Listen, I have to go out anyway." He doubted this was true but said nothing. "Let me return it and buy us an assortment of washers."

"There's a nice guy there who can help you. An older man. His name is Ernie."

Jennifer left right away. While she was gone, Richard studied the fix-it-yourself book like he was cramming for a final exam on the history of tariffs. By the time she returned, he had memorized all the steps involved in the job of removing and replacing a worn washer for a kitchen faucet.

He laid out the tools he needed the way the book said to do. He found the shut-off valve under the sink. He remembered to put a towel over the drain so none of the parts would go down it. He took a deep breath and removed the faucet's decorative cap. For the next half-hour, he concentrated on the several different steps for fixing a leaky faucet like a surgeon removing an appendix. And when he had finished and finally turned the water on and back off, he was astonished to see that the faucet didn't leak.

The garage door slamming shut snapped Richard back into the present moment. Turning away from the window, he saw that the moon appeared to be balanced at the very top of the maple tree across the street. He suddenly remembered the star atop the Christmas trees of his boyhood. He pushed this memory away.

He heard the back door open and close.

When he entered the kitchen and saw Jennifer, he stopped in his tracks. She looked exhausted. Her eyes were puffy and red. He didn't need to ask if she had been crying. A wave of guilt again washed over him. He wanted to apologize for not being with her today. But not now. Instead he asked, "So, would you like to get something to eat?"

She squinted at him for a moment and then said wearily, "Give me a few minutes."

CHAPTER FIVE
Sweet, Golden Honey

I T NEVER TOOK LONG for Richard to become impatient when waiting for Jennifer to get ready to go out. But this evening, he was glad for the chance to sit on the living-room couch and think things over. As he did, he realized he had been over-reacting for the past few days. He chuckled softly at what he now saw as his foolishness. Taking Heidi to Fillmore College today hadn't been as important as he had made it out to be. If it had been, Jennifer would have been upset with him the moment he walked into the kitchen. She had been a little tired, but that was only to be expected. Everything was fine.

He stretched out on the couch and made himself more comfortable. They had been married for more than twenty years. She had long known about his quirks. She had hers, too. Everyone has quirks. But they had come to accept each other for what they were. And Heidi? She was too busy tonight making new friends to give her father so much as a passing thought. He had wasted a couple of days worrying over nothing.

He was getting hungry. His appetite had been off for the past few days. Now he felt the way he did after a stomach bug had run its course and food had once again become palatable.

In his increasingly serene state of mind, Richard was all the more taken aback by Jennifer's frown when she finally appeared. He told himself not to say anything. She had probably been dreading this day for months. He shouldn't expect too much from her. Heidi's absence must be hitting her even harder than he had thought it would. Comfort food at their favorite diner was the answer.

"Want to go to Sunny Glen?" he asked.

"Sure, that'll be fine," she replied, her tone clipped by a hint of impatience.

"I'll drive," replied Richard, hoping she would see this as a thoughtful gesture.

They got in the car, and Richard turned on the radio as they backed out of the driveway. He turned the dial to an oldies station they both enjoyed. Chad and Jeremy's "A Summer Song" was playing. Perfect timing! One of their all-time favorites. He had always thought it was the prettiest song to come out of the sixties. This would cheer Jennifer up. He turned the volume knob to the right.

"Please turn that off," said Jennifer.

"But this is our song!"

"Richard, I don't want to hear it!" Her voice was shrill, almost a shriek.

Stunned, Richard did as she commanded. They drove in silence for a few blocks. He glanced over at her a few times. Her eyes were closed. He couldn't be sure if she had fallen asleep.

"Are you alright?"

"I have a headache," she said without opening her eyes. "I need to have it quiet for a while."

The only sound the rest of the way was the drone of the car's tires on the road.

The breakfast, lunch, and dinner menus at Sunny Glen had remained the same from the day the diner first opened in 1958. Waitresses had always worn the same emerald-green uniforms with starched white aprons. The laminate countertops with the boomerang design were the same as they had been on the first day the restaurant opened. Richard had brought Jennifer to Sunny Glen on their first date, a few weeks after they had both graduated from the University of Connecticut in 1972.

Sunny Glen was crowded as it routinely was around dinner time. The familiar scent of French fries and melted cheese greeted them as they opened the door. It was a smell that always reminded Jennifer of going to the beach in Rhode Island during the summer when she was a kid and getting lunch at a little snack bar right on the edge of the sand. However, tonight, she didn't notice anything at all when she walked inside.

Waiting for a booth could sometimes mean waiting a quarter of an hour or more. But tonight, they'd walked in at just the right moment, when nobody was standing in line in front of them. Luckier still, a young couple with a baby were just getting up as Richard and Jennifer entered. All three were dressed in official, matching Boston Red Sox jerseys. The mother carried her child wrapped in a Red Sox blanket, and the father was carrying a Red Sox duffle bag slung over his shoulder.

Richard gave the father a thumbs-up and said, "Nice jersey!"

The young man beamed and returned the thumbs-up. So did his wife. They were an attractive couple. Jennifer wished she knew who they were as they walked out. She wondered if she would ever see them again. *Probably not.*

Since nobody was waiting in front of them, they sat down at the booth the young couple had just left. Jennifer sat where the young mother had been. The seat was still warm. A wave of loneliness swept over her. She peeked at Richard's expression. *Is he sad that he'll never have the chance to know that lovely young couple and their baby? Does he, too, wish he knew the baby's name? Does he also wish he could hold the baby, even for a few seconds?* She wished he did. Then she wouldn't feel so alone; she'd have someone to share her loneliness with. But as Richard scanned the menu, it didn't appear to her that he felt sad at all.

A tall young woman efficiently cleared the plates, glasses, and napkins the young family had used. Richard glimpsed the nametag pinned on her uniform: Suzanne. She beamed a warm, friendly smile, first at him and then at Jennifer. As she wiped off the table, she asked Jennifer about her day. Jennifer smiled faintly in her direction but said nothing. Suzanne, her pencil poised above her small, spiral-bound notebook, waited for their orders. Jennifer handed her back the menu and ordered what she always did at Sunny Glen: the cheeseburger special.

Richard held the menu in front of him without seeing it or anything else in the restaurant. All his attention was focused on Suzanne. She was beautiful. Everything about her was perfect: her eyebrows, lips, freckled nose, sculpted arms, sandy blond ponytail spread across her left shoulder. Her exquisitely proportioned curves.

He unabashedly took in all of her loveliness. She turned to him, her mouth slightly open in such a way, it seemed to him, to either ask him for his order or to give him a kiss. In that moment, he was hopelessly smitten.

"Have you had a nice summer?" he found himself asking before Suzanne could speak when she turned to him. Both women blinked at him in surprise. Any other time, their reactions and the subsequent reddening of his face would have mortified him. Now he didn't care. All that mattered was the sound of Suzanne's voice speaking only to him.

"Why, yes, I have, very much so; thank you," she answered. Her voice was sweet, golden honey flowing from a burnished goblet. Her eyes were the blue of the sky on a bright, crisp winter day.

In his enchanted state of mind, he didn't realize he was staring at her. Jennifer did. She studied Suzanne up and down in a glance. The reason for the ridiculous look on her husband's face immediately became apparent to her. Admiration and resentment for the lovely young waitress clashed in her mind. Her headache returned in a flash.

Richard, do you have any idea how puerile you look? But can I blame him? My God, this girl should be modeling in New York City. When was the last time my husband looked at me that way? Did he ever?

It wasn't unusual for Jennifer's friends to tell her how attractive she looked when they went out to lunch together. Though she brushed off the compliments, they always made her feel good about herself. And when she looked in the mirror, she knew her friends weren't just being nice. She watched what she ate, faithfully exercised three times a week at the gym, got at least eight hours of sleep every night, drank plenty of water throughout the day. None of her friends came close to fitting into the same dress size they wore in college. But she could. And when she showed up at a picnic or dinner party wearing one of her outfits, she sometimes detected a delicious trace of jealousy in her friends' voices.

But now it was Jennifer who was tasting the acrid bile of envy. She couldn't hope to compete with a woman half her age, at least not one who looked like—she glanced at the name tag on the emerald-green uniform—Suzanne. She suddenly felt every minute of her forty-four years. At least twice Suzanne's age!

"And you, sir?" asked Suzanne.

"Yes, I've had a very nice summer," he replied. "Thank you for asking."

All he could see were Suzanne's momentarily confused eyes focused on him as if he were the only person in the diner. For that reason, he didn't notice Jennifer glaring at him in disbelief.

"Oh, I'm happy to hear that," said Suzanne in her honeyed voice. "But what I meant was, what will you be having to eat tonight?"

Returning reluctantly from his orbit around Earth, he asked for the Sunny Glen Special: their celebrated cheeseburger, hand-cut fries, coleslaw, and a large glass of Coke. Not until Suzanne thanked him and walked away did Richard notice Jennifer scowling at him through narrowed eyes. Apparently, her headache still hadn't lifted. He wished he had some aspirin to give her.

Their food came to them with the always-quick service Sunny Glen was known for. Suzanne made sure they had everything they needed. Richard was certain he saw a fleeting wink in his direction as she turned away from him. The more he thought about it, the more convinced he became that she had just sent him a coy little message. This possibility thrilled him so much that he didn't even try to contain his beaming grin. He didn't notice Jennifer's grimace as he took a king-sized bite out of his cheeseburger.

Their conversation was limited to an occasional comment about seeing someone they recognized or a request to pass the ketchup bottle. Jennifer tried to ignore Richard whenever he cast a surreptitious glance around the room.

It's as if I'm not even sitting here. Does he think I'm blind? Maybe he thinks I'm stupid. Maybe he's forgotten I'm even here. He'd like it if I weren't, wouldn't he?

Even more than good food and fast, friendly service, Sunny Glen was famous for its wide variety of homemade ice-cream flavors. People came from miles around for a mint-chocolate-chip cone, a metallic dish with a scoop of peach melba, a cookies-and-cream milkshake, or a hot-fudge sundae.

Just as they finished eating, Suzanne appeared at their table. "Did you leave any room for dessert?" she beamed as she collected the dishes, expertly balancing them on her strong right arm. The look on Richard's face as he gazed up at Suzanne was too much for Jennifer to endure. She glared at her fingernails rather than watch him continue to make a fool of himself.

"Let's have two hot-fudge sundaes," he said, without asking Jennifer first. This time, there was no doubt in his mind that Suzanne had, once again, winked at him. A technicolor vision appeared before his eyes. He was young again. Suzanne was his, and he was hers. Going to the movies . . . walking along the beach at sunset . . . candlelight dinners . . . weekends at a ski lodge . . .

"Richard, are you even listening to me?"

Richard glanced up to see Jennifer leaning forward, staring at him intently.

"Of course," he exclaimed so loudly that the people in the next booth over peeked at him. He tried to read the meaning of her expression. "Sure I am," he said more softly.

Suzanne arrived just then with their hot-fudge sundaes. Jennifer again scrutinized her nails. Richard desperately wanted to say something to make Suzanne laugh. He longed to hear the sound of her laughter, yet no joke or witticism came to mind.

Suzanne strode briskly away to another table without so much as a glance in his direction.

Richard slumped down in his seat. He had been fooling himself. He was just another customer to her. She probably smiled at every guy his age the way she had at him.

Neither Richard nor Jennifer reached for a spoon. Several seconds passed as they both stared down at the table, each lost in their own very different thoughts.

"There's something I need to say to you," said Jennifer, her voice barely above a whisper. Richard raised his head and blinked a few times. "Did you notice I was a little late getting back tonight?" She didn't wait for his answer. "I didn't come straight home from dropping off Heidi this afternoon."

Richard, too filled with pity for his decrepit middle-aged self, said nothing. Jennifer paused to consider what she should say next. She was tired, and she had a headache. Perhaps it would be better not to say anything until next morning. Yes, she would wait until later for a better time.

But just as Jennifer made this decision, Suzanne strode past them, carrying two chocolate milkshakes. Richard picked up his spoon and waved it at her like a flag. Jennifer's eyes narrowed when she saw this.

"I stopped at a grocery store that had a pay phone by the front door," she said, her voice cold and hard.

"You made a phone call?" he responded finally, sounding weary and defeated.

Jennifer straightened her back, took in a deep breath, and looked her husband squarely in the eyes.

"I called Peter."

She could see this wasn't registering with him. "I called your father," she said. Her own voice sounded strange to her, like it wasn't hers.

Just like that, she immediately had his full attention.

"You stopped at a pay phone on the way home and called my father?"

"That's right."

"Why?" He rubbed his hand across his face as if trying to awaken from a dream. "I mean, what did you talk about on a pay phone—with my father?"

"We talked about a lot of things," said Jennifer. She hid her hands under the table so Richard wouldn't notice how much they were shaking. "I got a ten-dollar roll of quarters from the clerk in the store. Peter and I had a lot of catching up to do."

Richard shook his head in bewilderment.

"There's something else you should know." She hesitated, and then she caught another glimpse of Suzanne's radiant smile as she waited on a couple in a booth just behind Richard.

"I invited your father to join us for the Labor Day weekend. At the cottage." Her voice, constricted by anxiety, sounded to her like the squeak of a frightened mouse. "He was thrilled to be able to finally see it."

For a second, she wasn't sure if he was going start yelling at her right in the middle of Sunny Glen. Instead, he reached into his rear pants pocket and produced his wallet. He opened the wallet, took out two bills, and tossed them on the table. Then, without speaking another word and without eating a spoonful of his sundae, he arose. Looking straight ahead, he marched out of the diner, leaving Jennifer sitting by herself.

She stared at the two bills, a ten and a twenty.

"That's some tip, Suzie," she muttered under her breath. "You certainly know how to play middle-aged men, don't you?"

She also left her sundae untouched.

As she followed her husband out of the diner, Suzanne beamed a smile and waved goodbye to her. The pretty young waitress appeared puzzled as Jennifer, stone-faced, proceeded quickly out the door without returning any friendly gesture of her own.

Neither Richard nor Jennifer spoke a word on the ride home.

CHAPTER SIX

The Song of a Whippoorwill

LATE AFTERNOON HAD always been Richard and Jennifer's favorite time of day at the cottage. They both loved the hours when the sun lowered over the hills beyond the lake and its yellow rays glistened on the water. The wind would die down, the air would become still, and the quiet would be like a benediction for the day.

On this day, however, the beginning of Labor Day weekend, with dusk drawing near, there was no sense of peace at the cottage. Jennifer and Richard had hardly spoken a word to each other in a week. When they had found it necessary to speak, it had been only in terse fragments.

The drive to the cottage was usually an exciting time, full of anticipation and excitement. But now, especially without Heidi chattering away in the back seat, the silence had become more strained with every passing mile.

By the time they had arrived at the cottage, the tension had become, for Jennifer, all but unbearable. As she carried in a bag of groceries, she realized she couldn't take the strain much longer. It was time to break this standoff between her and her husband. If it had to be her to do this, then so be it.

After talking herself into it, she strode resolutely into the living room, where Richard was sitting in his rocking chair by the bay window, reading a newspaper. Holding two neatly folded blankets close to her like a shield, Jennifer waited for him to acknowledge her presence. She cleared her throat. His only response was to turn to the next page. She cleared her throat again, a bit more loudly. He lowered the paper and shot a glance in her direction. Before he could raise the paper back up, she pounced.

"I'd like to ask a question," she said, enunciating each word slowly and carefully, as if English were her second language.

Richard lowered his newspaper again just enough to glare over the top of it at her. "Yes, what is it?"

Jennifer sat down on the couch, clutching the blankets tightly. He raised the newspaper back up, reestablishing a barrier between them. Unnerved by her husband's hostility, she forgot why she had entered the room. She tried to think of something, anything, to say.

"Isn't that last week's paper?" she called out.

Once more, Richard lowered the paper. His voice was tight and clipped. "If that's your question, then the answer is yes."

He didn't even try to conceal a sneer as he ducked back behind the newspaper. Jennifer struggled against a wave of rising hurt and anger surging through her. She didn't want their entire weekend ruined. Especially this one. After several seconds, she calmed herself enough to answer him. "No, that's *not* what I wanted to ask you."

When he didn't reply, she went on as if he had. "I've been thinking about changing the rooms. Well, not changing the rooms themselves, but changing them so that our bedroom will be Heidi's room and we'll get hers." She paused to let her words sink in. Richard again failed to respond, so she continued. "Heidi's room is actually a little bigger than ours. So is her closet. I've been thinking for a while that we should make that change. Now that she's away at college, this seems like the right time."

She paused again, a little longer this time, to give him a chance to react. Just when she'd concluded that he wasn't going to respond to her, he mumbled from behind the newspaper, "Heidi hasn't moved to Antarctica. I don't want to take her room from her."

It was the most he had said to her at one time since the evening at Sunny Glen. As if on cue, words that had been building up like a logjam all week now came tumbling out of her, bumping into one another as she spoke. The loosening of a few allowed all the others to flow forth.

"It's more than just that. I was thinking your father would like to stay in that room while he's here, since he's never been to the cottage before. I thought it would be nice for him to wake up and see the lake the first thing in the morning . . . just like we have so many times over all these years."

She paused a third time, hoping for some kind of reply, anything to let her know what effect, if any, her words were having on him. But her shoulders slumped when he remained closed off from her. She lowered her head in surrender. "We can always go back to the way things were later," she said in a subdued tone of voice, "since he'll be here for only a few days."

Richard lowered his paper deliberately and again glared at her. She stared right back at him. A long-forgotten childhood memory of staring contests with her big brother, Bill, came to her. She had always won those contests. And she won this time, too.

Richard threw the newspaper down on the floor. He twisted around with his back to her and stared over his shoulder at the lake. His posture reminded Jennifer of Heidi's childish way of pouting years ago when she didn't get her way. The ticking of the clock in the kitchen resounded throughout the cottage. After what seemed to her an interminably long time, he turned back to face her again.

"I guess you make all the decisions around here now. Is that it?" he asked, his voice dripping with sarcasm.

She gripped the blankets even more tightly. Refusing to take the bait from him and flee from the room, she forced herself to speak calmly. "No, it's for *both* of us to decide."

"Oh, of course—this is still my place, too. Silly me."

"That's why I'm running it by you first."

He rubbed his hand over his face and stared intently at the ceiling. *What is he searching for up there? Something he lost?* She resisted the temptation to ask.

"'Run it by me first,'" he mimicked her with a caustic chuckle; then he added, with a sneer, "Why couldn't you do that before you invited my father here?"

"Because I knew you would say 'no.'"

He hadn't expected such a straightforward answer. Stymied by this candid response, he could only stare at her, his mouth slightly agape. He reminded Jennifer of the straight man in a Three Stooges short. A grin darted across her face before she could catch it; she quickly wiped her hand across her mouth and again looked him in the eye.

"Like I said, we could just try it and see. We can always go back to the way things were if it doesn't work out."

Richard continued staring past her as if she weren't there. Jennifer realized there was nothing more she could say. At least nothing he would listen to. She got up from the couch and took a few steps away from him.

"You keep saying that," he muttered.

She spun around to face him, eager to receive any opening he might give her. "I keep saying what?"

"That we can go back to the way things were," he grumbled. "It wouldn't be that big of a deal," she said, taking a tentative step back toward him. "All we have to do is move—"

"We can never go back to the way things were!" he interrupted, his voice rising with each word until he was shouting at her. "And in the future, have some courtesy. Ask me first before you extend any invitations!"

Her eyes narrowed; her face flushed crimson. She took another step toward him, still clinging to the blankets. They were now up to her chin. Any higher, and they'd cover her face.

"And *you* ask me first what I want before you order dessert!" she yelled.

Richard's jaw dropped in bewilderment. If she hadn't been so upset, Jennifer would have laughed at how foolish he again appeared.

"What are you talking about?" he demanded.

"You know perfectly well what I am talking about."

"I have no idea what you're talking about."

She hovered over him, scowling down as he glared up at her.

"You did everything but ask that girl out on a date!" she sputtered.

"What girl?"

"As if you don't know 'what girl'!"

He eyed her defiantly, his jaw set tight, his teeth clenched.

"The waitress at Sunny Glen!" Jennifer cried out.

"You mean—Suzanne?"

His eyes widened as he realized his error. He tried to hide his blunder by glowering all the more as she smirked down at him.

"I see you remember after all. It looks like the lovely Suzanne made quite an impression on you, didn't she?"

"That's ridiculous," mumbled Richard, struggling to recover from his misstep. "I didn't ask her out on a date."

"I didn't say you did. But, oh, you wanted to. You were so pathetically obvious with your goo-goo eyes and childish prattle."

"You're crazy! I was just being friendly—that's all."

"Sure you were. Like the friendly tip you left her."

He was fighting a losing battle, and he knew it. "You're just trying to change the subject."

"And what exactly is the subject?"

He sprang to his feet in a rage. Her stomach heaved. She felt she was about to throw up. He stepped back, his anger smothered by a surge of remorse when he saw the fear in her eyes.

"The subject," Richard said, struggling to remain calm, "is you having the—audacity—to invite my father here. Without my permission!"

"Since when do I need your permission to do things I want to do?"

He took in a deep breath. "Okay, fine. Wrong word. My approval—my say so—my input—whatever the word is, you had no right to do that behind my back."

"Richard, the next few days could be a happy time for us if we let them."

"In all the time you have known me, what has ever made you think that would be possible?"

He was still fuming, but now she also recognized the sadness of a little boy in his eyes. Clutching the blankets ever tighter to her chest, she took a cautious step toward him as he stared blankly down at the floor.

"Would you please tell me once and for all what the problem is between you and your father?" she asked gently. He responded to her conciliatory tone with another outburst.

"Oh, no you don't! We are not getting started on this again," he snarled. He took another deep breath in an attempt to compose himself.

"We have *never* 'gotten started' on this," said Jennifer, trying as hard as she could to stay calm. "Every time I've ever tried, you've cut me off right away."

"Exactly! That's why you should have known to ask me first. Before inviting my father! And here, of all places! The one place in the world where I find some measure of happiness!"

Like a volcano about to erupt, Richard's anger mounted with each word. Without realizing it, he sprayed Jennifer with his spittle. He observed a rivulet coursing down his wife's cheek. It took him a second to realize it had come from his own mouth.

Before he could apologize, Jennifer turned and lurched away from him. With the blankets up to her chin and partially obscuring her vision, she didn't notice the coffee table. The outside of her calf scraped against the table's sharp edge. As though from a distance, she heard a woman scream and a man yell out her name. Tumbling headlong out of control, she hit the floor so hard that the wind was knocked out of her with a sickening *whoosh*.

Before Jennifer fully understood what had happened, she felt hands on her shoulders. Someone turned her around gently and helped her sit up. She took in a mouthful of air but couldn't fill her lungs. A shock of panic surged through her. She felt someone gently patting her back and heard whispering in her ear. She took in a full, deep breath, and her mind cleared. She became conscious of her leg throbbing with pain.

Jennifer glanced down at her calf and noticed blood trickling down in a little stream toward her ankle. Already a little red pool had formed as her blood dripped onto the floor. She became lightheaded and shut her eyes tight.

"I'm so sorry, Jen," Richard moaned, close to tears. He helped her to her feet, guided her over to the couch, and supported her as she lay down. He placed the couch pillows under her leg and rushed out of the room. He returned with an armful of towels, his hands filled with a bottle of hydrogen peroxide, a tube of ointment, and a metal container of Band-Aids.

Jennifer watched as he placed a towel over her cut and pressed against it tenderly. As Richard stared at the towel, she had the otherworldly sensation she was watching a movie of a man tending to a woman's wound. Whose blood-smeared leg was that? Who was this man holding a white towel smudged red to the woman's leg? Where were they? Jennifer vaguely realized she was slipping out of consciousness. She asked for a glass of water. Richard brought it to her at once.

After a minute or so, Richard gingerly removed the blood-stained towel. He used a clean towel to dab lightly at her injured calf. Then he put the towel down, bent forward, and examined her cut.

"I don't think you'll need stitches," declared Richard as he straightened up. The calmness in his voice reassured her. For the first time in days, he sounded like her husband again.

She peeked at the wound. Feeling faint again, she quickly turned away and shut her eyes tight. After a second, she opened them and saw Richard peering at her. A tiny smile crossed his face. He motioned for her to take a look. She nodded, took his hand, and squinted at the wound. This time, she didn't look away.

"It's not as bad as I thought it would be," said Jennifer. "I thought I had broken my leg at first."

Richard carefully washed the cut with the peroxide and another clean towel; then he delicately dabbed the antiseptic ointment over it. He applied the bandage with meticulous care. When he was finished, he helped her to sit up. He placed a pillow on the coffee table and slowly lowered her leg onto it.

He's being so gentle. Is this the same man who has hardly spoken to me in a week?

Richard sat down on the opposite end of the couch and covered his eyes with his hand. He looked exhausted. Or was he just contrite? Jennifer couldn't tell. A minute passed, perhaps a bit more or a bit less. She reached over and softly touched his arm.

He turned to her. With a toss of her head, Jennifer motioned him closer. As though he had been awaiting this signal, Richard immediately slid over to her until their sides were touching. She brushed her hand across his. He took hold of it with both of his. The softness of her hand made Richard remember the first time he had held it. It had been a warm evening in October of 1971, less than a week after meeting her one rainy Saturday afternoon in the nearly deserted UConn library when the Huskies had been playing a football game against UMass in Memorial Stadium. They had been walking back from a concert in Von der Mehden Hall after listening to Vivaldi's *The Four Seasons*. Richard had reached for her hand and missed, clutching only her pinky finger. He tried again and secured her hand tightly in his. He had not held another woman's hand since.

Without saying another word, they gazed out the bay window at a sunset of yellow, orange, and red cirrus clouds hovering over the lake. The colors reminded Jennifer of the chrysanthemums she and Heidi had seen at the entrance to Fillmore College.

"Did I really make that big a deal?"

Jennifer didn't respond. After several seconds, he added, "Over Suz—that waitress? At Sunny Glen."

"I know who you meant."

"Well, she *was* kind of pretty," he said, straining for a credible air of nonchalance. A nervous little chuckle gave away how he really felt. He attempted a smile but couldn't hold it more than a second before it contorted into a grimace.

"Suzanne wasn't pretty," said Jennifer.

He shot her a glance to see if she was being serious.

"Richard, she was gorgeous."

"I guess sometimes—" he paused, searching for the right words to express himself. Twice more he tried to speak but stopped in frustration. When he had difficulty expressing himself, Jennifer would usually help him put his feelings into words. Not this time.

Richard finally gave up. The two of them returned to silence as they viewed the brilliant colors of the sunset. Like the embers of a dying campfire, the vivid yellows and reds gradually faded away into somber shades of gray over the lake.

"I guess I don't always understand," he began—and then stopped himself again. He ran his fingers back and forth through his hair. He turned to her, shrugging in defeat. Jennifer nodded but still said nothing to come to his assistance.

He shook his head in exasperation.

What's irking him? Something about himself or me? She willed herself to remain silent as the room gradually darkened more and more. When he finally moved, Jennifer thought he was getting up to turn on a light. Instead, she could barely make out that he had turned to face her.

"I guess I don't always understand how I'm coming across to others." Just at that moment, the lonely song of a whippoorwill came from somewhere in the woods behind the cottage. "Do you understand what I'm trying to tell you?"

"Richard, I was humiliated."

He hadn't expected to hear *that.* His stomach knotted up in anticipation of a coming rebuke. But then he noticed she hadn't let go of his hand. If anything, she was holding it all the tighter. He leaned his shoulder into hers.

"I'm sorry," he said softly, and then she rested her head on his shoulder.

"I'm sorry, too. I should have spoken to you first before inviting your father."

Soon the lake, surrounded by the black perimeter of the woods, reflected the last muted gray light of the waning day. The sound of crickets filled the air.

"Someday it'll be too late to say anything to your father," said Jennifer, giving his hand a squeeze.

"I know."

"I don't want you—I don't want *us* to live with that kind of regret."

He started to say something but stopped.

"I miss Pop," she said. It had been such a long time since she had used that name for her father-in-law in front of him. "I didn't realize just how much until recently."

Keeping hold of Richard's hand, Jennifer leaned over and turned on the lamp by the couch.

"Listen, his train isn't due at the station until 4:30 tomorrow afternoon," she said. "If we leave here by 4:00, we should make it to the station in plenty of time. That will give you most of the day to go fishing."

When he didn't reply, Jennifer got up and stiffly bent over to pick up the blankets off the floor. Before she could reach down, Richard jumped up and gently took them from her. "I'll help you refold them," he told her as he handed her one of the ends. She smiled at him when they saw the blanket was tangled. He smiled wanly back at her as they started over and folded the blanket into a neat, precise square. They did the same to the second one, each grateful as they worked to see the other smile at their slightly bumbled efforts.

"I'm going to go lie down in bed and read a little," she said.

"How's your leg?" he asked.

"I'm okay," she fibbed as she walked out of the room, trying with all her might not to limp. He was relieved to see her appearing to walk normally. She peered around the bedroom door. "It's probably best if we don't change the rooms for now. Maybe some other time."

"I'll be coming to bed in a minute," was all he said.

Instead, Richard spent the rest of the evening sitting on the couch staring out the bay window in the direction of the darkened lake. Her leg elevated slightly by a spare pillow, Jennifer read a novel until she fell asleep with the book sprawled across her chest.

CHAPTER SEVEN

A Game of Scrabble

J ENNIFER AND PETER HAD been talking ever since
Peter had stepped off the train. But just as they
were finishing dessert, silence descended upon the room, making
the hot, muggy air seem even more oppressive. Jennifer glanced
at Peter as he gazed pensively at his wine glass. She peeked over
at Richard, who was staring straight ahead, his chin supported by
his folded hands. The dark circles under his half-closed eyes made
him look so weary that Jennifer thought he might fall asleep at any
moment. What had he done during the day to tire himself out?
Her thoughts wandered back to several hours earlier.

Peter and Jennifer had greeted each other at the railroad station
with beaming smiles as soon as their eyes had met. Peter had let
his suitcase fall on the concrete platform to reach out to Jennifer
as she approached. They had embraced each other warmly. Peter
expressed concern about the bandage on her leg and the limp she

had not entirely been able to hide from him. "I'm fine," she said. "Just didn't watch where I was going."

Peter went to hug Richard, too, but sensing his son was not going to respond in kind, he extended his hand instead. With a forced smile and a curt "Hello," Richard shook hands stiffly with his father. At Jennifer's urging, Richard picked up Peter's suitcase. All the way to the car, he had walked a few steps behind his wife and father. On the half-hour ride back to the cottage, Richard hadn't said a word. Jennifer and Peter, barely pausing for breath, had chatted about the weather, the Red Sox, and the coming school year the entire time.

When they got back to the cottage, Richard had gone straight to his black-walnut rocking chair by the bay window. After Peter had settled in, Jennifer grilled steaks while Peter shucked several ears of corn. In spite of the uncomfortably steamy air, the two of them had laughed and talked while setting the kitchen table together. When everything was ready, Jennifer called out to Richard, who had been sitting there the whole time, holding a book as if reading it. Jennifer caught herself before asking him if he had finished so much as a single paragraph.

While they ate, Richard's only contribution to the conversation had been perfunctory replies to Peter's questions. Jennifer had had to bite her tongue to keep from complaining about her husband's rudeness. She kept glancing over at Peter each time Richard had responded tersely to his father's attempts to start a conversation. The older man's gentle demeanor and even tone of voice had never once faltered.

❧

Jennifer broke out of her reverie when Peter remarked in his soothing baritone voice, "Richard must have told you that steak and corn on the cob are two of my favorites."

Thoughts flashed through her mind like heat-lightning over the lake. *No, he hasn't told me what you like. He hasn't told me anything about you. Ever!*

She glanced up to catch Peter's gentle blue eyes studying her. He blushed and looked away. Richard's eyes were deep-set like his father's and the same color. She had noticed that about her husband years ago. But until this moment, she'd never detected the same melancholy in Peter's eyes that she had seen so often in Richard's. She felt herself absorbing the mutual sorrow of the two men, the osmosis of some personal grief whose origins were unknown to her.

"Who doesn't like a good steak?" she responded, forcing herself to sound cheerful.

"Tenderloin no less," said Peter. "And silver queen corn!" He held up his wine glass, and Jennifer clinked it softly against hers. He turned to eye Richard with an eagerness that brought Jennifer to the verge of tears. She watched as Peter raised his glass tentatively in his son's direction to toast the just-finished meal with him as well, but Richard gave no indication of even noticing his father's gesture. Instead he poured more wine into his glass and swigged it down in one gulp. Peter reluctantly lowered his glass back down onto the table.

Witnessing this latest example of her husband's insensitivity was too much for Jennifer, and she leapt up from the table so abruptly that both men were startled. She attempted to deflect her angry reaction with a smile, but her smile twisted into a grimace. Embarrassed by her appearance, she hurriedly started to clear the table. Peter picked up his knife and fork as he rose from his chair.

"Pop, you stop that. Put those down right now!" ordered Jennifer. Startled, Peter's hand froze in the direction of Richard's place-setting. Her head spun from getting up so quickly. She held tight to the edge of the table for a moment to steady herself as she reached for a plate.

"I guess the heat's made me a little woozy," she said, half expecting Richard to tell her it was her third glass of wine, not the heat, that made her wobble. But her husband refrained from saying a word.

"Sorry, I didn't mean to sound so bossy. I was just practicing my teacher's voice for the new school year," she said brightly, hoping this would reassure Peter she wasn't upset with him. She shot a glance at the object of her annoyance. He was staring down at the table, oblivious to everything and everyone around him.

"I just want to do my share," replied Peter as he resumed reaching over for Richard's knife and fork.

"No, Richard and I will take care of it. We want you to relax while you're here with us." She turned to her husband. "Isn't that right, Richard?" she said, unable to entirely conceal the edge in her voice. He rose obediently, without giving any other indication he had heard her.

The three of them carried the dishes and utensils to the kitchen sink, leaving the not-quite-empty wine glasses on the table. Richard and Peter waited compliantly as Jennifer filled the sink and a yellow plastic dishpan with hot water and then squirted some soap into the sink. Richard gingerly lowered his dish and utensils into the water; then he turned without a word and shuffled his way out of the kitchen. He settled with a soft grunt into his rocking chair, his back half-turned away from them.

"Tell you what," said Peter when he noticed Jennifer biting her lip. "You wash, and I'll dry. How does that sound?"

Jennifer nodded, reached into the soapy water, took out a plate, and ran a sponge across it. She handed the plate to Peter, who rinsed it off in the dishpan and placed it in the rack to dry. The hot water made the oppressive air that much clammier. They stood so close together that their shoulders bumped as they cleaned and rinsed, cleaned and rinsed.

"Thanks, Pop," she said as Peter placed the last knife in the rack. "It was fun washing dishes with you. That sounds a little silly, but it's true." She gave him a spontaneous little hug around his shoulders. His shy smile told her he appreciated the gesture. She made a mental note to hug him as often as she could over the next few days.

"I always enjoy accomplishing something," he said, "even if it's something as mundane as a household chore."

"Is that how you stay young?"

He put his finger up to his lips and made a shushing sound.

"That's the secret. But don't tell. I'm putting it all into a book," Peter whispered in a confidential tone. He chuckled when he saw Jennifer wasn't sure for a moment if she should believe him or not.

They sat back down at the kitchen table. Jennifer, fanning herself with a folded newspaper, noticed the several inches of wine still left in the bottle. She poured some for herself and went to pour the rest in Peter's glass, but he held up his hand to refuse it.

"I've had enough for one night," he asserted. "It's excellent, but I don't drink all that much wine anymore, so it doesn't take a lot to make me tipsy."

Jennifer put the bottle down without taking the rest of it.

"I enjoy a good glass of wine now and then," continued Peter, wanting her to know he appreciated her generosity, "but it's best when enjoyed with someone you love. Since Sarah died seven years ago, I just haven't felt festive enough . . ." His voice trailed off.

Richard, while careful not to get caught eavesdropping, had listened to their every word since sitting back down in his chair. His eyes screwed up in pain when he heard his mother's name mentioned. "Mind if I have the rest of that wine?" he asked.

"Of course not," replied Jennifer. Hoping her husband might rejoin them after all, she poured what remained of the chardonnay into Richard's glass. He got up from his rocking chair and approached the table as Peter and Jennifer both smiled at him. But instead of acknowledging them, he picked up his glass and drank the wine in one last gulp. He then walked back to his rocker, as if there were no one else in the room but him, and sat back down, with another grunt.

I'd have sent Heidi to her room in a heartbeat if she acted like this, Jennifer thought. *Not that she ever would have.* She willed herself to ignore what she saw as her husband's utter lack of manners and to focus all her attention instead on her father-in-law.

"How has life been treating you, Pop?" she asked. She noticed Richard tossing an irritated glance in her direction when she once again addressed his father as "Pop."

I've had it with you. Sit over there by yourself and stew for the rest of the night for all I care, she thought.

"Just fine," replied Peter. "Never better than at this moment."

"Tell us about yourself," insisted Jennifer. "What have you been up to since we last saw you?"

Peter made a face that looked as if he had just bitten into a lemon.

He doesn't want to say a word about himself, thought Jennifer. *Like father, like son.* But unlike Richard, Peter responded instead of storming out of the room when asked a personal question.

"There's not much to tell when you live in a retirement community. Oh, it's pleasant enough—very nice, actually. I'm fortunate to have landed where I am now."

Peter started to say more but instead straightened his back and clasped his hands together with an authoritative clap. "But enough about me! What I really want to talk about is all of you!" he said in a cheerful, though commanding, voice. "First, tell me all about my favorite granddaughter."

Jennifer glanced at Richard to see if he would be willing to answer his father's question. Not a chance. He seemed deeply engrossed in the latest edition of *Field and Stream*.

"I—we—took Heidi to her college last weekend," she said, as brightly as she could manage.

Peter interrupted her before she could say more. "I had the most delightful conversation on the phone with her about a week ago. The night before she left for school."

"Did you know that, Richard?" Jennifer asked.

"What?" asked Richard. He glanced at them as if just now noticing that they were in the room with him.

"Did you know Heidi called your dad the night before she left for school?"

Richard's eyes narrowed, and his lips pursed as if searching his memory. He nodded at her. "Yeah, I guess I do." He went back to his magazine, flipping quickly through several pages.

"Has she thought about a major?" asked Peter, looking in his son's direction. The pause lasted long enough for Richard to look over and see that the question had been directed to him.

"Everything from architecture to zoology," answered Richard as if this were common knowledge, hardly worth the mention. He immediately turned back to his magazine again.

"Of course!" exclaimed Peter. "She's exploring all her possibilities. That's the very best thing she could do at this time in her life. I know she'll succeed in whatever she finally decides to do.

You two have raised a wonderful daughter. I'm sure you're both very proud of her."

Richard turned for a moment to his father with a tight-lipped grin, lacking any trace of warmth. It vanished as soon as he returned to his magazine. He continued to flip through pages with barely more than a glance.

"And I'm proud of you both for doing such an excellent job as her parents," said Peter, his eyes fixed on Richard's profile. Richard made no move to acknowledge his father. Peter turned to Jennifer and asked her, "And how has life been treating you two lately?"

"We've been doing okay," she responded, pausing on the last word with an inflection that caused Richard to glance for a second in her direction. "It's a bit different now without Heidi around." She paused. "It's kind of a big adjustment." She bit her lip to keep from saying what she really felt. *It's devastating.*

Jennifer missed her daughter constantly. At the same time, she wanted Heidi to live her own life, to pursue her dreams, to be her own person. This conflict gnawed at her day and night. She definitely did not feel "okay."

The sun skirted just above the treetops bordering the lake's western shore. A cool breeze often came off the water at this time of day, but now the air was as sweltering as it had been at noon. As Jennifer considered the sunbeams sparkling on the lake, that same end-of-summer melancholy she had experienced the day she took Heidi to Fillmore College swept over her again.

She looked over at Richard, sitting in his rocking chair. In his mid-40s, he had achieved the middle-aged distinction of a slight paunch. He was graying just a bit around the temples. She had always thought of herself, and therefore her husband, as being young. But seeing her husband's age starting to show, she realized she had to face the fact that she, too, was getting older.

She was gripped by a sudden urge to grab Peter's hand, get into the car, and drive with him to Fillmore College. It was just a few hours away. Heidi would love to see her grandfather. And he would love to see her. Jennifer shivered with both excitement and apprehension as she pictured this actually happening.

"Listen to those crickets. They're so loud out here in the woods," said Peter, breaking into her thoughts. "I've heard crickets all my life at this time of year, but for some reason they remind me this evening of when I was a boy."

Jennifer placed her hand over Peter's and gave it a squeeze. He squeezed back. She was surprised at how strong his grip was. His hand was also moist with sweat. Was this because of the stifling heat or because he was anxious? *Had inviting this sweet man to the cottage been a good idea after all?*

"This is my favorite time of year," she said with the same air of brightness, as she tried to push away the thought that this weekend might turn out to be a huge mistake. *My huge mistake.* "The air is crisp, and the light is softer now than in the middle of summer. The trees will soon turn colors. I love that it's getting close to autumn."

Peter closed his eyes and cleared his throat. In his warm baritone, he recited:

> "Season of mists and mellow fruitfulness,
> Close bosom-friend of the maturing sun;
> Conspiring with him how to load and bless
> With fruit the vines that round the thatch-eves run;
> To bend with apples the moss'd cottage-trees,
> And fill all fruit with ripeness to the core;
> To swell the gourd, and plump the hazel shells
> With a sweet kernel; to set budding more,

And still more, later flowers for the bees,
Until they think warm days will never cease,
For summer has o'er-brimm'd their clammy cells . . ."

When he didn't continue on, Jennifer spontaneously applauded. "That's all of it I remember," murmured Peter. "My fifth-grade teacher, Miss Plimpton, loved poetry and had us memorize a poem a week. I used to hate it, but ever since then, I've been glad she made us do that."

"You recited it beautifully," said Jennifer. Peter nodded his thanks to her. He turned to Richard, who had, despite appearances, listened attentively to his father's every word.

"I'm grateful to have this chance to see your cottage," said Peter. Richard gave no indication he had heard. Peter spoke more loudly. "I'm sure you've had many wonderful experiences here over the years."

Richard still did not respond. Unable to keep silent for another moment, Jennifer spoke up. "Thanks. We've loved it here. And Richard has been making improvements since the day we moved in."

Peter acknowledged her with another nod and turned back to his son again. "Is that right? You've done some very good work, then. I'm especially impressed with the claw-foot bathtub. Was that one of your projects?"

Richard nodded slightly and Jennifer noticed his rigid expression soften into the merest trace of a smile. In the time it takes for a lightning bug's flash to go dark, his smile vanished. "It wasn't all that much," he said flatly, without returning his father's steady gaze.

"That's not true at all!" exclaimed Jennifer, hoping flattery might draw Richard out of his shell. And, she told herself, it wouldn't really be flattery since everything she could say would be true. "Richard had to learn how to do everything from scratch, but he did all the plumbing for the bathtub, including the shower assembly." Her brow furrowed in concentration as she tried to remember other jobs he had successfully undertaken over the years. "And he replaced the steps leading up to the deck!" she added triumphantly.

"I'm very impressed," marveled Peter. "I didn't realize you had such skills."

Richard tried to refocus on his *Field and Stream*, knowing his father and wife were still watching him with hopeful anticipation.

"If you think I can ever help you out in some way in the future, just let me know," Peter added a little shyly.

There is that half cord of wood to be stacked and covered before the weather turns cold in a few weeks, thought Richard. For a moment, he was tempted to take his father up on his offer. He could use the help, especially with the way his middle-aged back had been acting up recently. "Thanks, but I'm all set," he answered brusquely.

This abrupt reply smothered the possibility of any further talk for the next minute. In the stillness, the distant honking of geese grew steadily louder and more insistent. Jennifer got up from the couch and walked a bit stiffly over to the picture window.

"Is your leg feeling any better?" asked Peter. Hearing the concern in his voice, Jennifer answered him with a thumbs-up and a grin. She hoped this would keep him from guessing from the way she moved how much it actually stung.

She peered out the window at clouds stretching like ribbons of gold and red over the lake. "Oh, look—there they are!" she said after several seconds. She pointed toward a wedge of geese silhouetted against the sky. "Right over Big Moose Island! They're flying in a perfect V!"

Peter got up and joined her by the window. With their backs now to him, Richard lowered his magazine and squinted over his shoulder. "They're flying south for the winter," said Peter. "Another reminder of change."

"Some things never change," muttered Richard before he could stop the words from escaping his mouth. Peter turned toward him. Richard felt like his father could look inside him and see the confusion roiling about in his brain.

"What do you mean, Richard?" Peter asked.

"Nothing, just an expression," answered Richard. He had no idea why he'd said that. He kept his mouth shut tight for fear of what else might come flying out from it. Trying to distract himself from his father's tight-lipped, piercing gaze, he thumbed through his magazine, each page a blur. He was relieved when he saw, out of the corner of his eye, his father turn back again to look out the window.

"Look! There's the evening star, right above the tall pine tree on Big Moose Island!" Jennifer cried out. Peter followed the line to where her finger was pointing.

"Yes, I see it," said Peter. In a sing-song voice, Jennifer repeated the nursery rhyme she had once recited to Heidi at bedtime years ago. At the sound of the first word, Richard bowed his head and closed his eyes, as though in prayer.

> "Star light, star bright,
> First star I see tonight.
> I wish I may, I wish I might,
> Have the wish I wish tonight."

Jennifer's eyes lingered on the star for another second, and then she turned to Peter. "I made a wish. Did you?" she asked him.

Peter, his eyes fixed on the star, nodded. "Yes, I did," he said solemnly.

Jennifer turned to ask Richard the same question. With his eyes closed, he nodded his head and whispered, "Yes."

"Good, now all our wishes will come true. That still happens, doesn't it, Pop?"

Peter smiled faintly at her. She saw that same trace of sadness in his eyes. He turned to Richard. "Your mother used to recite that poem to you and—" He cleared his throat. "—to you at bedtime."

"She did?" asked Richard with a sudden interest that caused Peter and Jennifer to simultaneously turn to him.

"Oh, sure," answered Peter. "Do you remember?"

For the first time since Peter had stepped off the train at the station several hours ago, Richard looked directly at his father. "No, I guess I don't," he said, matching the melancholy in his father's voice.

Once again, silence descended on the room, making the sultry air even more oppressive. After several moments, Jennifer spoke up with a somewhat exaggerated cheerfulness.

"Anybody up for a game of Scrabble?"

"I haven't played Scrabble in many years," said Peter with a chuckle, "but I'll give it a try."

Jennifer, aware of her injured leg, knelt down cautiously to the bottom shelf of the bookcase and grabbed the game. "How about you, Richard?" she asked.

"Not tonight," said Richard, as he searched for another magazine in the wicker basket by his chair.

"You're just afraid of getting beat—again," said Jennifer playfully as she got the game set up.

"Yeah, that's it," replied Richard as he found a *National Geographic* and leaned back. He thumbed through it, once again hardly looking at the pages. Jennifer stared in his direction, trying to get his attention.

"I'd better warn you, Pop," said Jennifer as she turned to him. "I'm pretty good at this game. Just ask Richard."

Richard continued to turn pages rapidly.

"Just take it easy on an old guy who doesn't have all his marbles," chuckled Peter. Jennifer saw the faintest glimmer of a smile flash across Richard's face.

"Richard, are you sure you don't want to play?" she asked, emphasizing the last word in a way that she knew would get his attention. His eyes darted to her for a second, and she tilted her head, raised her eyebrows, and, in that same instant, winked at him.

He recognized this look of hers at once. It was the same one that had told him many times over the years: "Trust me—you and I are about to have fun!" It was the look that had preceded picking apples on a September afternoon, roaming through flea markets, building sand castles at the beach, planting and tending to a vegetable garden their first summer of being married. And now, it came as an invitation to play a game of Scrabble. He had never been able to resist these alluring commands of hers. Tonight was no exception. With a shrug of his shoulders, Richard got up from his rocking chair and joined them at the table.

Jennifer shook the cloth bag holding the letter tiles a few times, opened it, and held it out for Peter to take the first seven letters. She did the same for Richard; then she took her own letters. "You go first, Pop," she said.

They each looked over the letters in their wooden racks. Jennifer moved the tiles around a few times while Peter stared at his letters intently. Richard sat holding his chin in his right hand, appearing bored. His boredom soon turned to frustration as the silence amplified the sound of water dripping from the kitchen faucet into the metallic sink. The more he tried not to listen, the louder each drop became.

Peter picked up one of the tiles from his rack, hesitated for a moment, and then placed a Q on the center space. He deliberately picked up one tile at a time to form the first word of the game: QUIETER. Jennifer stared wide-eyed at the board. Richard did a double take but said nothing.

"That's a pretty good start for an old-timer," said Peter under his breath.

"Yeah, it sure is," said Jennifer as she added up the points. "Double letter on the Q, plus double for the first word, plus a 50-point bonus for using all your letters! Let's see," she said, adding up the point totals on her fingers. "That gives you a total of 102 points!"

"Beginner's luck," said Peter. He seemed a little embarrassed by such a good start.

"*That* is a tough act to follow. Do you want to go next, Richard?" asked Jennifer.

"No, you go ahead," mumbled Richard.

"The champion has taken a hit," Jennifer said, mimicking a color analyst for a Sunday afternoon football game. "Can she recover? The crowd is hushed."

Richard shook his head and scowled in exasperation as Jennifer played a word. He reached for a napkin to wipe away the sweat on his forehead. Jennifer put down her word: READY for seven points.

"That's the best I can do for now," she said as she reached into the cloth bag for four new letters. Your turn, Richard."

Richard turned back to the board and stared at it glumly. The art deco wall clock, shaped like a starburst, next to the refrigerator, ticked off a full minute.

"Are you planning to put down a word sometime this evening?" Jennifer asked, not quite able to conceal her annoyance.

The metallic ticking of the clock continued for several more seconds until Richard raised his head and regarded her with a blank expression. "Do you have to catch a bus?" he replied stonily. He again stared down at the board with the same dull and empty demeanor. Jennifer tapped her fingers lightly on the table. When she noticed this was annoying him, she tapped a little louder until she saw Peter staring at her. She stopped at once.

Trying to distract herself from what she took as Richard's passive-aggressive behavior, Jennifer glanced around the room. She noticed cobwebs in the corner by the refrigerator. *How had I missed them? Damn, I thought I had cleaned the house thoroughly.*

As she considered whether to get the long-handled duster and sweep the cobweb away, a large moth flew into the room. It circled frantically around the light above the sink and bumped against the ceiling. The moth fluttered to the window screen above the sink, thumping against it with a sound like a tennis ball being thrown.

"Wow, that's a big bug!" exclaimed Peter.

Richard glanced up, his eyes widening as he followed the moth's deranged flight. Jennifer stared at Richard as the moth struck the screen over and over. Seeing he wasn't going to bother getting the moth out of the house, she rose from her chair and rolled up a newspaper. Trying to corner the invader, she lunged at it with a grunt and missed awkwardly. Peter burst out with a laugh that sounded more like a sneeze and then snorted at the sound he had made.

Jennifer swung away over and over at the moth. Pausing to take another swipe at it, she noticed Peter and Richard watching her. Their open-mouthed expressions of astonishment told her how ridiculous she must look. Giving up any last remaining shred of her dignity and ignoring the pain in her leg, she lashed away wildly at the moth as she limped around the room, chasing after it. After a few more seconds of this spectacle, even Richard couldn't keep from laughing.

Jennifer circled the moth as if it were an opponent in a boxing ring. Finally, she managed to corral the insect near the screen door. Flinging open the door, she swung so hard at the moth that she lost her balance and fell on her injured leg. The moth flew out the door. She yelped out in pain and let go of the door, which slammed shut with a loud *thwack!* Richard jumped at the sound as though a gun had gone off behind his ear.

Peter leapt to his feet to help Jennifer get up off the floor. He led her by the arm back to her chair. Her beet-red face streaked with sweat, she fell heavily onto it. Neither of them noticed the mounting distress in Richard's face. His eyes darted back and forth as though as he were trying to find a way out of the room. A bead of sweat trickled off his face onto the table in front of him. A few more seconds passed until Jennifer, the pain in her leg finally lessening, exhaled and said, "Okay. Your turn, Richard."

When he didn't respond, Jennifer turned to him. Her expression morphed from puzzlement to concern and finally to alarm. Before she could ask him what was the matter, Richard swept his hand across the board. The board tipped over and sent the tiles flying about the room. Peter and Jennifer stared in shock at Richard. He gawked back at them, as dazed by what he had just done as they were.

"Richard, what are you doing? What's the matter with you?" sputtered Jennifer.

Richard stared open-mouthed at his wife and then at his father. He had no answer to her question. He sprang up from his chair and paced back and forth, both hands so tight over his mouth he appeared to be trying to suffocate himself. They watched in stunned silence until he at last stopped pacing and turned to them.

"I have to go out for a moment—for a walk." He turned toward the door, flung it open, and hurried outside.

"Do you want a flashlight?" Jennifer called after him. *What a ridiculous thing to ask*, she thought. She and Peter stared at the open door and listened to the crunching of Richard's shoes on the gravel walkway as he trudged off into the darkness. Peter turned to Jennifer.

"I wonder what's the matter with him," Peter whispered, more to himself than to her. "Do you know?"

Jennifer bit down on her lip to keep from shouting at him.

Me? Do I know what's the matter with him? That's what I want to know! You're his father. Tell me what's wrong with my husband!

The question she had wanted to ask for years pushed its way to the front of her mind. She tried to push it back down, as she had done for years with Richard. But the question had waited too long. It demanded to finally be brought out into the open. Before she fully realized what she was doing, Jennifer heard herself asking him what she had kept to herself since the first months of being married: "Why don't you and Richard get along?"

Jennifer had wondered in the past where and when she would ask Peter this question. *It turns out on a steamy September evening in the cottage.* She felt like she had entered a forbidden room and opened a box that was meant to stay sealed forever. Her anxiety increased with every second the question hung in the air. The crickets sounded to her like they had entered the house and were surrounding her. She had always loved to listen to their late-summer song, but now the sound was incessant and made her all the more nervous.

"I really can't answer your question," Peter replied at last in a matter-of-fact tone. "Once, a long time ago, there used to be ball-playing in the backyard, going to the beach, Christmas presents, hugs, laughter. But all that was a long time ago when they—when Richard was just a boy. Who knows why things turn out the way they do?"

Peter shrugged his shoulders and stroked his chin.

"I can't remember the last time Richard really shared a genuinely happy moment with me. It had to have been before—"

This weekend is all a terrible mistake after all. I never should have invited him here.

Just then, Richard's footsteps announced his approach to the cottage. Jennifer and Peter saw the relief in each other's faces as he walked up the steps and opened the door. He stood by it, appearing to be unsure about whether he should walk through it or not. Jennifer half expected him to bolt out into the darkness again at any moment.

"Dad, I'm sorry—" Richard began at last. He stared at them as they sat staring back at him, nobody knowing what to do or say. Before another word was spoken, he rushed to the bedroom, slamming the door behind him.

"Richard!" called Jennifer after him. She ran to the bedroom, yanked opened the door, went in, and closed it behind her with a bang. Expressionless, Peter remained seated, staring at the closed door. He then rose and bent over to pick up the Scrabble tiles scattered throughout the kitchen. Far off in the distance, thunder rumbled through the sultry air as a cold front slowly approached the lake.

CHAPTER EIGHT
The Man in the Boat

OVERNIGHT, THE COLD FRONT swept in over the region around Big Moose Lake. The clinging stickiness of the past several days was washed away by the torrential rains and swirling winds of a series of thunderstorms. They arrived one after the other through the night, like waves breaking along a darkened shoreline. The last rumble of thunder died down to a distant whisper as the first rays of the morning sun transformed lingering clouds from the storms into dazzling ribbons of red, orange, and yellow. Everything was now smooth and cool to the touch. The air was fresh and clean, scented with pine trees.

The aroma of fresh-brewed coffee greeted Jennifer as she walked into the living room after her morning shower. She was dressed in her bright-pink bathrobe with a matching towel wrapped around her wet hair like a turban. She stifled a yawn with the back of her hand.

She had not slept well. After Richard had gotten ready for bed, he had given her his customary bedtime peck on the cheek and, as he had been doing for the past several years, immediately turned on his side away from her. Adding to her aggravation, he had fallen asleep in less than a minute as if filled with contentment after enjoying a pleasant family evening get-together. It had been all she could do to resist the urge to grab his shoulder, shake him awake, and demand an explanation for what had happened.

Whenever she had closed her eyes, she had seen Scrabble tiles whirling around her. At one point, seconds after at last falling asleep, she had dreamt that a Scrabble tile was heading straight for her eyes. Her body had jerked spasmodically to get out of the way. Wide awake after that, her neck muscles tightening until she had a headache, she had listened for what seemed like half the night to Richard's deep, rhythmical breathing. And when sleep finally began to settle over her, the first clap of thunder reverberating over the hills around the lake startled her awake again.

When Jennifer entered the room, Peter was sitting on the couch so deeply engrossed in a book that he didn't notice her presence at first. She saw he was dressed comfortably for an autumn-like day. His light-blue jeans and green plaid long-sleeved shirt would have been much too warm to have worn the day before.

She sighed with gratitude upon walking into the room and being greeted by the scent of freshly ground coffee. Her spirits lifted for the first time since the Scrabble pieces had gone flying around the kitchen.

"Good morning. Thanks for making coffee," she said softly so as not to startle Peter before he became aware of her presence. He turned to her, smiled a greeting, and returned at once to the book. She walked over to the old-fashioned coffee percolator on the stove top. Seeing Peter had a cup already by his side, she poured herself one and sat down on the couch next to him. She tried to curl her legs under her, winced in pain, and sat with her feet on the floor.

"What's that you're reading?" she asked.

Peter turned the front jacket toward her so she could see it. "Bruce Catton's marvelous book: *Never Call Retreat*. It's the last volume of his trilogy on the Civil War."

"'The Civil War'—that's something like what we had here last night," said Jennifer, looking over the cup as she held it up to her mouth with both hands. He looked at her quizzically and then scowled when he realized what she was referring to.

"Oh, I don't know if I'd call last night's little incident a 'war.' That's not what war is at all." Hearing the disapproval in his voice, Jennifer quickly changed the subject.

"Did you bring that book with you?" she asked.

"No, actually. I found it here," he replied. His face relaxed, much to her relief.

Jennifer put down her coffee. "May I look at it for a second?" she asked. Peter handed her the book. She skimmed through it, reading just a few sentences here and there, before handing it back to him. "I usually prefer fiction when I read for pleasure."

"Yes, I enjoy a good novel, too," said Peter. He paused, not sure for a moment if he should finish his thought. "I wish I could say this book was fiction. I'd just finished reading Catton's account of the Battle of Fredericksburg when you walked in. What a terrible battle that was. I wish all war were just a fiction created in the mind of an author. That's the only way war could ever be acceptable." Peter's voice trembled slightly as he said this. She changed the subject again.

"Those thunderstorms last night finally broke the heat," she said as she took an orange out of her robe pocket and began peeling it. "Did they wake you?"

He shifted his posture. She saw he was still ill at ease. She began to wonder if he were feeling well. *Perhaps last night's little incident is bothering him more than he's letting on.* He answered her with a slight nod, indicating they had.

"I always enjoy a good thunderstorm," she said, trying to sound bright and cheerful. "And the ones last night brought good sleeping weather with them."

"Hmmm, I suppose they did."

Jennifer had been about to share a slice of the orange with Peter but stopped when she noticed he was squinting out the picture window toward the lake. The lines around his eyes were more deeply etched. He suddenly looked older to her.

"Did you sleep okay?" she asked him softly. "Except for when the storms woke you, I mean?" He shrugged, still staring fixedly out the picture window.

"The mattress wasn't comfortable enough for you, was it?" Jennifer asked, raising her eyes to the ceiling in aggravation. "I *told* Richard we should replace it!"

"The mattress was fine," he replied, turning toward her and managing a smile. "I always have a difficult time sleeping in a new bed for the first time."

"Have you been sleeping well at home?" she asked, realizing that she might be asking too many questions for his liking. "Tell me the truth, now."

He hesitated long enough for Jennifer to feel her stomach tense up. But when he finally answered her, his voice was calm and level. "If it's the truth you want, I've been having strange dreams for the past few months that wake me up, and then I have a hard time getting back to sleep."

"Did you have strange dreams last night?"

Peter rubbed his thumb across age spots on the back of his hand as if noticing them for the first time.

"Yes. The thunderstorm must have triggered them. That's happened before."

"Have you gone to see a doctor?"

He studied her, slightly bemused. "Now, really. What am I going to tell a doctor? That I'm having scary dreams?"

Her eyes riveted on him with no hint of a smile.

"I'm fine, really. There's no problem at all."

"What kind of dreams are you having?" she asked.

"Oh, now, I shouldn't have said anything," said Peter.

"No, that's not true," Jennifer insisted. "I don't want you to keep things from me. I get that sort of thing enough from Richard."

He reached over and patted her hand gently. "I assure you I'm just fine. If anything is ever wrong, I'll tell you."

"Promise?" she asked, scrutinizing him for the slightest twitch.

"Scout's honor," he said, holding up the three middle fingers of his right hand and covering the nail of his pinky in the Boy Scout salute. She mouthed the word "okay" and then offered him a slice of her orange. He took it, and they ate the rest of the fruit one wedge at a time, each content not to speak until they had finished.

The cool, dry air, the coffee filling the cottage with its familiar, comforting scent, and the sweetness of the orange all gave Jennifer a sense of much-needed contentment. She imagined her back and neck muscles melting into the couch cushions, the way she had learned in her meditation classes. She closed her eyes and listened to the morning breeze gently rustling through the pine trees surrounding the cottage.

When she opened her eyes again, Jennifer glanced over at Peter and saw he was once again staring out the picture window in the direction of the lake. She turned around and arched her back to see where he was looking.

She immediately caught sight of Richard, alone on his boat, fishing in his favorite little cove about forty or so yards away from the shore. As always when fishing, he was wearing his battered old sou'wester fisherman's hat. He wore it in both sunshine and rain for the luck he believed it had given him ever since the day, years ago, when he caught five largemouth bass in one morning.

Seeing the faded red flannel shirt he refused to throw away and a pair of jeans with holes in the knees, Jennifer wondered what his high school students would think if they could see the always-impeccably dressed Mr. Franklin looking like a—well, bum. But did she really know him any better than his students did? As she regarded the man in the boat, a man she had spent more than half of her life with, it dawned on her that she couldn't say for sure if she did.

Sometimes when Richard was fishing, she would take out her crocheting and work on one of the sweaters she gave as Christmas gifts. She had given so many sweaters to family and friends that, several years ago, she began to crochet them for people at the local homeless shelter.

Over the years, she had come to associate her crocheting with Richard's fishing. She imagined that the two of them were sharing a peaceful time that made them both happy. So even though they were not actually together, they were still sharing a common experience.

This suddenly struck her as a strange, even desperate way to think about her marriage. Had she created some kind of pathetic trick of the mind to comfort herself? Had she devised a clever way to coexist with a husband who could be so aloof and distant, who so often escaped into his own private world?

She had never seen her marriage in quite this way before. A tear trickled down her cheek at this realization. She quickly brushed it away so Peter wouldn't see. This was not the time for any tears.

Jennifer managed to stanch her tears, but the thoughts that had generated them were not as easily dismissed. She had struggled constantly not to call Heidi since she had dropped her off at Fillmore College. She had written to her faithfully since, forcing herself with each sentence not to mention to Heidi how much she missed her. Every day, she had resisted the temptation, after she put a letter in the mailbox at the corner of her street, to go back home and write another.

"There's my boy," said Peter, breaking into the thoughts coursing through Jennifer's mind.

"I guess I was hoping—" began Jennifer, catching herself as she realized what she was about to say.

"He might have invited me along with him?" asked Peter, finishing her thought. She could only shrug her shoulders.

"That would have been fun," said Peter, speaking so softly Jennifer could barely hear him. They watched together as Richard reeled in his fishing line and then expertly cast it again into the center of the cove.

"We used to go fishing together," continued Peter in the same soft tone of voice. "But that was a long, long time ago."

Jennifer desperately tried to think of something, anything, to focus her attention on, to deflect the tears she could feel about to burst out of her if she couldn't find a way to fend them off.

"Let's go to Infinity!" she declared eagerly, turning to Peter with the wide-eyed expression and breathless excitement one might see in a child who wants to go to a parade.

"Infinity?" he asked incredulously, not sure if he had heard her correctly.

She felt a little silly upon seeing the puzzled look on his face. *He must think I'm scatterbrained.* "I'm sorry. You don't have any idea what I'm talking about. 'Infinity' is the name I've given to a big rock outcropping right at the edge of the lake. There's a place where the rock has been shaped into a large hollow almost like a lounge chair. It's big enough for two or three people to sit in. I like to go there and look out over the lake. It's so comfortable I've sometimes stayed there for the better part of an afternoon. When I'm there, I feel the Earth is holding me like a baby in her arms."

"Sounds lovely," said Peter. "I'd like to see this special place of yours. It's a great morning for a walk. Would you show it to me?"

"It's less than five minutes away. We could go whenever you like. As soon as we've had some breakfast, that is."

"We could have breakfast when we get back, if you'd like. Let's go right now and work up a little appetite."

Jennifer was already hungry, but even more, she wanted to get out of the cottage as quickly as possible. From Infinity, they wouldn't be able to see Richard fishing in the cove. An empty stomach was preferable to staying inside, where she would be forced to see Richard keeping himself apart from them.

"Let's go, then," said Peter, putting his fist up against his mouth to stifle a yawn.

"You're tired," she observed. "Maybe we should go later."

"No, I'm fine," protested Peter. "Like I said, it's a lovely morning for a little walk. The fresh air will wake me up."

"Let me get dressed, and we'll go. I know you'll love it there as much as I do."

"I'll read a little more of Catton's book while I'm waiting for you."

Jennifer got dressed quickly. She decided to take along a sweater against the morning chill. As she walked out, she took two apples from the basket by the door leading out to the deck and put them in her windbreaker pocket. She hesitated for a moment and then snatched two more.

CHAPTER NINE

A Soldier's Final Resting Place

O NCE THEY WERE OUTSIDE, Jennifer and Peter found the morning air brisker than they had expected. They were both glad they had dressed for a day that had dawned more like autumn than summer.

As they walked along the narrow path leading to Infinity, Jennifer's hand brushed against Peter's hand for a moment. She considered taking it in hers, but then decided against it, not sure how Peter would feel about such intimacy.

He pointed to some crimson at the top of a tree. "You can see the first of autumn color in some of these leaves," he said.

"That's a red maple; they're usually the first to turn. It seems to happen earlier every year," Jennifer replied.

They continued along as the wind rustled through the trees. A few leaves fell around them, the first of a multitude soon to follow. When they came to a fork in the path, Peter started down the trail leading to the lake, which shimmered in the morning sun.

"Not that way, Pop," said Jennifer, pointing in the direction they should go. Peter halted, but, before turning back to her, he noticed something peculiar just off to the right ahead of him, about twenty-five yards away. Amid the bushes and trees, he could just make out a row of thin, straight lines fixed in place, unaffected by gusts of wind.

"That's an old graveyard," said Jennifer when she saw what had caught his eye. "It's always seemed to me an odd place for one. It's not like those buried here need the view of the lake."

His eyes darted around to the surrounding trees. "I'm sure this is all second-growth forest. Probably would have been farmland around here at one time."

"I guess that hadn't occurred to me before," nodded Jennifer. "Why else would a graveyard be out here in the middle of the woods?"

She took a step on the path leading to Infinity but stopped when she saw Peter still staring in the direction of the cemetery.

"Would you like to take a closer look?" she asked.

"If you wouldn't mind," he responded, though he wasn't sure what was compelling him to want to.

The rectangular cemetery was roughly twenty-by-thirty feet. It was surrounded by a four-foot-tall wrought-iron fence made of slender columns spaced several inches apart. The columns, pointed like spears, were rusted and covered with lichens and mosses. They protected a half-dozen or so headstones scattered throughout the enclosed space.

Jennifer and Peter slipped silently inside through the gateway, as though entering a church. They wandered reverently among the stones, trying to decipher the weatherworn words engraved on them.

"It's difficult to read what's written on these stones," said Jennifer.

"The markers are probably made of limestone," said Peter, walking toward a stone that had been broken in half. "It carves well but tends to fade over time from the weather."

"O-ba-di-ah," sounded out Jennifer, stopping at one of the stones and kneeling to get a closer look. "I can't make out the last name. It looks like it begins with a 'P-O.'"

"I think I saw a Porter's Farm Road near here yesterday," said Peter.

"Yes, that's right!" exclaimed Jennifer. "It's the main road off the dirt road to the cottage. You were right, Pop—this must have all been farmland at one time. Isn't that fascinating?"

When Peter didn't reply, she looked up to see him kneeling in front of the severed gravestone as though he were praying before an altar. His hand was covering his mouth, and his brow was knitted in concentration as he stared fixedly at the stone. She went over to him. Peering over his shoulder, she read what remained of the inscription on the stone:

Porter

1839

Killed at Fredericksburg

December 13, 1862

"Fredericksburg," she said. "We were just talking about that back at the cottage. In the book on the Civil War you were reading."

"Yes," he said. He moved a little closer to the stone, reached out his hand, and ran his fingers over the word "Fredericksburg."

"Do you think perhaps the person buried here might have fought there?" asked Jennifer.

After a moment, Peter looked up at her. "That's likely, I'd say. Many of the men killed in the Civil War were buried on or near the field of battle. It appears this man was among the fortunate ones whose bodies were brought home," he said, nodding solemnly. "His family have to have been well-to-do to be able to afford the expense. The Porter farm must have been unusually productive."

"What a terrible thing, to bring your son back from a far-off battle in a box," said Jennifer.

"Yes, it's terrible when young men are killed in war," said Peter, not taking his eyes off the broken stone. "And Fredericksburg was one more terrible defeat that year for the Union Army. When Lincoln heard the news of the battle, he said, 'If there is a worse place than hell, I am in it.' It was hell, alright—all war is." He swallowed hard before continuing. "I knew of a battle like that."

"Tell me," she said.

"During the war—World War Two." He waved his hand as if swatting away a mosquito. "But so did lots of guys."

Jennifer felt her stomach tighten. As always, something was being kept from her. Only now, it wasn't Richard but his father who was brushing her off. "I wish I had known before now. Richard has never told me anything about what you experienced then," she said. *Or much of anything else about you for that matter.*

Peter picked up on the hint of impatience in her voice.

"He wouldn't have known," said Peter. He started to get up. Jennifer took hold of his arm and helped him. "Thanks. My knees aren't what they used to be." He brushed off his pants and looked at her. "And the last thing you need to hear on a beautiful day like this is an old guy telling you war stories. The only thing more boring would be sitting around watching carrots grow," he said, forcing a laugh.

"Okay, but if you'd ever like to tell me about it sometime, I'd be happy to listen."

He once again began to wave off her offer as if it were a pesky insect but then caught himself when he saw a fleeting glimpse of hurt in her eyes. "Jennifer, I'd tell you right this minute if there were something important to tell, but there isn't." She nodded, but he could see she wasn't entirely convinced he would.

"Come now, let's be on our way to Infinity." He thought about what he had just said and snickered. "That sounds like a funny thing to say, doesn't it?" he asked. He waited until he saw just enough of a smile cross her lips to tell him she was okay.

With Peter in the lead, they had taken only a few steps when he stopped and looked back toward the cemetery. Jennifer waited a moment for him to start walking again, but he remained where he was. He bit the tip of his tongue and squinted as though deep in thought, trying to remember something.

"Pop, are you okay?" she asked, and, when he didn't answer, she felt uneasy. "You've got to tell me what you're thinking," she said.

Peter was too lost in his thoughts to pick up on the distress in her voice. It appeared to Jennifer he didn't even notice her presence. He took a step toward her as if she weren't directly in front of him. Jennifer was forced to step aside as he walked past her and back to the cemetery. She expected him to turn around and tell her what he was doing, but he kept walking back to the graveyard, still not saying a word. For a moment, her father-in-law's strange behavior made her want to turn around and run back to the cottage. *But what's there? Nobody! Heidi's in college now. Remember?*

Peter went through the opening and straight to the grave of the Civil War soldier. Jennifer came up alongside him, looking for any clue that might reveal what he was doing. But he only stood peering down at the grave, his lips pursed and his eyes narrowed in concentration. He glanced around the little cemetery and then back to the grave. Jennifer, growing increasingly anxious from his peculiar conduct, forced herself to keep still and wait for him to tell her what was going on. Just when she thought she couldn't stay quiet a moment longer, he turned to her and said matter-of-factly, "I've been thinking."

Bewildered, Jennifer watched as Peter, like a minister getting ready to say a prayer, extended his hands toward the grave of the veteran of Fredericksburg. He held this pose a moment; then he turned to her and said, "This is the grave of an unknown soldier."

All Jennifer could do was nod in agreement as Peter's eyes roamed over the graveyard. He gazed up at the trees and then back down at the grave.

"I had a thought," he said, "but you'll probably think it's foolish."

"Try me," was all Jennifer could think to say.

"This is a soldier's final resting place," Peter said. "Someone should take care of this cemetery, make it suitable for a man who served his country." He raised his hands toward the sky as though blessing the broken gravestone. "As this man did," he announced to the surrounding trees.

"That's a good idea," Jennifer managed to say, unsteadily.

Peter turned to her. "It wouldn't take much more than a few hours here. Do you have a rake, maybe a pruner, and perhaps a scythe?"

"Sure, we have those. You'll need a good pair of gloves, too."

"Everyone deserves a decent final resting place," Peter said with a catch in his voice, "especially a soldier who fought for his country. It seems that way to me, anyway."

"Me, too."

Peter bit his lip. "Do you suppose Richard would mind if I borrowed his tools for a little while?" he asked.

Jennifer paused to clear a lump in her throat before she spoke. *It's like Richard is a stranger to him.* "Richard won't mind."

Peter's eyes brightened when she said this. "Perhaps I can get to work this afternoon, after lunch. If it's okay with you, that is," he said. Jennifer nodded to let him know it was.

"But first we have an appointment to keep at Infinity," he said with a soft, easy laugh.

Whatever's going on, he sounds like himself again. Jennifer smiled and, taking his hand, headed toward the lake.

CHAPTER TEN

A Rush of Tears

AFTER PETER AND JENNIFER had lunch, Peter left the cottage to go back to the little cemetery in the woods. He took with him the bamboo rake and pruning shears Jennifer assured him he could use. Before he walked out the door, she also insisted he wear one of Richard's bucket hats.

"No, I won't need a hat," he said.

"Yes, you will!" she replied firmly, once again using her teacher's voice with him. "It may be September, but it's still summer. You don't want to get a sunburn on your head."

"Are you insinuating I'm going bald?" he demanded, with mock indignation. He saw she was afraid she had offended him, so he snatched the hat from her and placed it so low on his head that his ears stuck out. Seeing she was still not sure of his feelings, he took off the hat and, with a flourish, bowed like an Elizabethan gentleman.

Jennifer laughed and reached for the hat to place it properly on his head. As she did, she noticed how much Peter's gentle gray eyes resembled his son's. She wanted to tell him this, but a little voice within her told her not to.

Jennifer insisted that Peter also take a canteen of water with him. Finally, satisfied that her father-in-law was well prepared, she watched from the front door as he walked down the path, balancing the rake and shears in either hand until he was out of sight. Turning to go back inside, she glanced across the lake. There was Richard in his boat, fishing in the cove, in what Heidi had called years ago his "lucky spot."

There had been a time when it comforted Jennifer to see Richard fishing in that location on the lake. If the wind was blowing across the water just right from the west, she could call out his name, and he would hear her all the way from the cottage. He would wave to her, and she would wave back. Today the wind was coming out of the northeast. There would be no point in calling to him. The wind wasn't right.

She watched him reel in and recast his fishing line to a different place in the water. A question abruptly barged its way into her mind: *Why do I sometimes feel closer to Richard when he's fishing than I do when he's right there with me in the same room?*

The question seemed to hover in the late summer air, stirring up all kinds of memories. During their first year or two at the cottage, she had looked forward to him returning from the lake. He would walk in the door after carefully putting all his gear away. Then they would often sit and talk about whatever came to mind. Sometimes they talked away the rest of the afternoon, until it was time for supper. Other times, they were content to sit silently together, a wonderful intimacy filling the hush that enveloped them.

Jennifer bit her lip as her memory demanded she recall everything about her life with Richard. After the first few years, the silence was not always intimate. More and more often, it would seem to her to be a barrier. She would rack her brain trying to think of how to carry the conversation past how the fish were biting that day. Some days, nothing she could think to say would break through to him. She would get discouraged when that would happen and go for walks to Infinity. More than once, as she sat on the rock outcropping, the sunbeams shimmering on the water had been blurred by her tears.

As time passed, Richard's sullen moods gradually made Jennifer apprehensive every afternoon when it came time for him to return to the cottage. She learned to recognize his state of mind from the moment he got out of his boat. As Heidi got older, if Richard showed the signs of being in a yet another funk, she would take her daughter for a walk or a swim. Sometimes she brought Heidi to Infinity and read aloud from *The Secret Garden* or *Alice in Wonderland*. Those shared moments were some of her favorite memories of days spent at the lake.

In the midst of these thoughts, anger suddenly and unexpectedly knotted up her stomach. *This is today, right now, not a time long ago in the past. Heidi isn't here. She's off at college. Starting her own life. Apart from me. I'm alone now.* Her jaw clenched tight. She glared across the lake as Richard placidly cast his line into the water again. Her vision blurred in a rush of tears. She swiped them away with the back of her hand.

"As if he even cares," she declared, knowing that only the surrounding trees heard her speak these words. "There he sits, off by himself. Keeping himself separate from me and his father. Why? Why does he act this way?"

Then an even more disturbing thought came to her.

Has he been fishing all these years as a way of escaping me? Maybe fishing never really mattered to him, after all. Perhaps he doesn't care if he caught a mess of fish or nothing at all. He'd often return just as sullen and aloof either way. Maybe catching fish wasn't the point to spending hour after hour off by himself on the lake for all these years.

All those days, year after year, she had looked out across the lake and seen him sitting in his boat. His hat would always be low over his eyes as he stared with seeming patience into the water. Jennifer had always thought he appeared the very picture of contentment. Until now. But, if he had, in fact, been content, perhaps it wasn't because he was fishing. *Could it be he was content because he wasn't—around me?*

Jennifer tried to dismiss this thought from her mind. Too late. The notion had already taken hold of her mind and wouldn't let go. It metastasized. Had she just seen the *real* reason he hadn't come with them to Heidi's school a week ago?

A childhood fear sprang up out of its hiding place and clenched her in its grip. She thought she had, with the help of therapy, locked the fear away years ago. But now, free from the room she and her therapist had placed it in, it had escaped and was rampaging through her. Her heart pounded, and sweat beaded up on her forehead just as when she had cut her leg yesterday.

Once again, she was a little child, alone, with no safe place to where she could flee.

Her hands shaking and her breath coming in shallow gasps, she bolted into the kitchen. She flung open the refrigerator door and took out a bottle of wine. Holding it tight by the neck so as not to drop it out of her trembling hand, she placed the bottle in a wicker picnic basket along with two plastic wine glasses. She headed back outside, and as she did, she caught a glimpse of herself in the rectangular wood-framed mirror by the door. Coming to a halt and gazing at her reflection, she recognized the childhood panic she saw once again in her own eyes.

She rushed outside, not thinking to close the door behind her. She kept her eyes on the ground to avoid the sight of Richard out on the lake.

Don't look at him! Whatever you do, don't look at him!

She walked a few steps and then, despite her leg throbbing in protest, broke into an awkward run and hurried from the lake and toward the graveyard.

CHAPTER ELEVEN

His Own Private Act of Devotion

B EFORE THE GRAVEYARD came into sight, Jennifer slowed to a walk and then came to a stop. She didn't want Peter to see her panting for breath from her sudden exertion and anxiety. As her breathing returned to normal, she gazed up at the leaves quivering around her in the breeze. Above the tops of the trees, puffs of cottony cumulus clouds drifted by.

She closed her eyes and followed the practice she had learned in her yoga class years ago. She breathed in deeply through her nose, held her breath, exhaled slowly through her mouth, and then paused before breathing in again. After a minute or so, she felt calm enough to continue on toward the cemetery.

With his back to her, Peter didn't see Jennifer as she approached the cemetery. The soft murmur of the windswept leaves muffled the sound of her footsteps. She stopped to watch him raking around the broken gravestone. He worked with great care, as if the ground were a living thing that might be wounded if he applied too much force. She smiled to see he was dutifully wearing Richard's floppy hat in the warm September sun.

Her smile turned pensive when she noticed again how much alike Peter and Richard appeared. Each had the same long, sinewy arms and legs and the same graceful, athletic way of moving. She took a step toward him, and a twig snapped under her foot, just loud enough to cause Peter to turn toward her. They were both startled—he by her sudden and unexpected appearance, she by a momentary sensation that she was glimpsing not her father-in-law but her husband.

Once again, Jennifer's eyes filled with tears. This caught her by surprise, and, annoyed with herself, she squinted tightly to hold them back. When she opened her eyes again, she saw that Peter's welcoming smile had turned into a look of concern. She realized, from the way she must look, that he probably had good reason to be worried. Why had she become so unexpectedly sad, when, only a few seconds before, she had been smiling? Once more, she fought against an urge to run back to the cottage. She compelled herself to take a step forward. Her eyes riveted on the ground before her, she took a step, another, then another. Her heart pounding in her chest, Jennifer raised her eyes only when she reached the cemetery gate.

Peter cocked his head, smiled uncertainly at her, and raised the rake to greet her in what appeared to her was something like a salute. She marched through the gate, hoping the smile she forced would somehow hide the tears still coursing down her cheeks. She started to brush them away with the back of her hand but then put her hand down. That would call even more attention to herself.

"Are you alright?" he asked.

"Oh, I'm fine," she replied, feigning a casual air. "My allergies always act up this time of year. One minute, I'm fine; the next, my eyes are watering, and I'm sneezing my head off."

"I wish I had known that," he replied fretfully. "I would have picked up some antihistamine at the drugstore before I came."

"No, really, I'm fine. I have something I take at bedtime." His facial muscles slowly became less tense. Seeing this, she felt herself relax, too. "It looks like things are proceeding nicely here," she said.

He looked around the cemetery and sighed with satisfaction. "Just a little raking has made quite a difference."

Jennifer put the wicker picnic basket on the ground and lifted the lid. "I thought we might celebrate your progress," she said, lifting the bottle of Chardonnay out of the basket.

"I don't know if I've done enough to earn a celebration," said Peter as she took out the two glasses and handed them to him.

"I say the time is always right for a celebration," Jennifer replied as she cut away the foil around the bottle rim with a butterfly corkscrew. She raised the arms of the corkscrew, pressed the tip into the cork, twisted it in, and pushed the wings down. Kneeling down to set the bottle on the ground, she lifted the cork out of the bottle with a soft, rewarding *pop!*

As Peter held the glasses, Jennifer stood up and poured halfway to the top of each. She took one and straightened her arm toward him. But instead of clinking his glass against hers, he turned toward the grave with the broken stone. "Here's to an unknown soldier," he said solemnly. They extended their glasses in the direction of the grave and then gently clinked them together with a high-pitched *ping!*

She poured herself another full glass, but Peter held up his hand to refuse any more for himself. "That might be a bit too much," he protested. "I'm a lightweight, remember?"

"Are you sure?" she asked coyly.

"Perhaps just a splash then," he answered, not wanting to say "No" to her. The bottle slipped a little in her hand, and she poured more than a splash. "I suppose I shouldn't waste it," he decided and finished the last drop.

Jennifer had planned to remain with Peter at the cemetery until he finished. She thought she might even help him if he was getting tired. But she was well aware of why she had come to be with him. It hadn't really been to keep him company or give him a hand. Her reason was more selfish than that: she just hadn't wanted to be by herself in the cottage.

Peter picked up the rake but made no move to use it. He stood where he was, apparently uncertain of what to do next.

He doesn't need your help. This is his own private act of devotion. He wants to get back to work, and you're keeping him from it. It's time for you to leave! Now!

"How much longer do you think it will take you to finish?" asked Jennifer, heeding this inner command despite her reluctance to return alone to the empty cottage. She placed the bottle and glasses back in the picnic basket.

"There's not that much more for me to do," he said. "I'd say a half hour at most."

She checked her watch. "Okay—see you then." She walked a few steps and called back over her shoulder, "Just don't push yourself too much."

"I won't," he replied.

He watched her walk away down the path until the trees and shrubs concealed her from view. No longer able to see her, Peter nevertheless continued to stare blankly in her direction for several moments. He was suddenly lightheaded. *Too much wine.*

He walked—a bit unsteadily—to the other end of the cemetery to where a pile of old leaves from autumns past had built up along the iron fence. He raked the dry ones on top with weak, superficial strokes. A pungent, but not unpleasant, odor of decay rose up to greet him as he got to the decomposing leaves underneath. These were thick and wet and harder to rake. In his increasingly lethargic state, Peter was compelled to take even shorter strokes. He wished he had a pitchfork; the thin prongs of his rake could barely move the soggy mass. He stopped to take off his hat and wipe the sweat from his eyes with his shirtsleeve. He was becoming so drowsy that he wanted only to lie down.

Just another minute or two. Then I'll rest.

He took in a deep breath, exhaled sharply, and attacked the sodden leaves again. After a few more swipes, the rake tines scraped against something solid. He bent down to take a closer look. He had come upon a large, flat stone. He ran the rake across it a few more times and saw what looked like words emerging. He attacked the leaves with a sudden burst of energy. Soon all the heavy, sodden leaves had been cleared away to reveal writing on the stone:

Here Lies
Our Beloved Son
Nathaniel
Born

Peter turned around to look at the fractured gravestone. *The top half that had broken off!* He bent down to pick up the stone. It was heavier than he expected. His grip slipped the first time he tried to grab hold of it. With a firmer grasp and grunting from the exertion, Peter managed to pry the top half of the stone free from the saturated ground.

Carrying it bent over at the waist like a prehistoric cave dweller, he dragged the stone between his legs toward the grave. After carefully laying the top half up against the bottom, Peter gingerly straightened up. As soon as he did, he saw stars shooting across his field of vision.

He grabbed ahold of the top of the iron fence. He slowly inched his way down until he was sitting with his back resting up against the fence. With the reunited stone directly in front of him, he read the full inscription:

Here Lies
Our Beloved Son
Nathaniel Porter
Born 1839
Killed at Fredericksburg
December 13, 1862

Struggling to keep his eyes open, he stared intently at the etched words in front of him.

"Hello, Nathaniel," he said aloud. "I'm Peter Franklin." He glanced around the cemetery. "I've tried to improve appearances here. I hope you like the way things look now."

He chuckled softly to hear himself talking to the stone as though it were a living thing that might answer him. As he stared at the stone, his chin descended until it settled on his chest. As soon as it did, his eyes snapped open. He fixed his eyes on the stone.

"It's not Arlington, like you deserve, but I did the best I could to make it look presentable. It's the least I could do for an unknown soldier. Like you."

His head again slowly lowered toward his chest, but as before, he jerked his head back up and spoke again to the stone. "You're not unknown anymore. I know you. You're my brother."

Once more, his head settled on his chest, but this time he didn't lift it back up. The warm sun, the wine, and all his exertion lulled him into a deep sleep.

CHAPTER TWELVE
The Same Nightmare

A GUST OF WIND BROKE A dead branch from a bough with a sharp cracking sound. Peter's eyes flew open. For a moment, he was unsure of where he was. He must have fallen asleep, but for how long? He didn't know. Grabbing hold of the rake for support, he struggled to his feet. Reclining on the damp ground had stiffened his joints. He cursed softly as he fought against the dull pain in his hips and lower back to stand.

Just as he straightened up, he heard footsteps crunching over the branches and twigs on the path. He turned toward the direction of the sound but saw nothing. Jennifer? No, it wouldn't be her. She would have called to let him know she was coming back. Richard? Out fishing on the lake. The footsteps drew closer. He still couldn't see anyone. Were his ears playing tricks on him?

Closer yet. Peter detected the familiar metallic tang of fear on his tongue. He told himself not to be silly. It was just Jennifer. Or perhaps it was Richard after all, coming to talk with him! Still, he could see no one. No familiar voice called out to him as the footsteps grew louder.

All at once, a man loomed before him, not as if he had emerged from the surrounding woods but as though he had been conjured from the air itself.

He was diminutive, with a finely chiseled face and a slight frame. He walked with an easy, graceful stride. His feet barely seemed to touch the ground. Peter judged him to be in his early twenties, certainly no more than a year or two over twenty-five. He wore blue overalls with a gray sack coat over a light-blue button-down shirt. Curly, dark-brown hair poked out from under his wide-brimmed straw hat. A maroon kerchief tied around his neck was partially hidden under his full, well-groomed beard. His eyes were pleasant and genial.

"Good day to you, sir," called out the man cordially in a high-pitched, reedy voice. Peter returned the greeting with a hesitant wave. The man rested a hand on top of an iron rod and glanced round the cemetery.

"You've sure been sprucing up this old place," said the man. Peter sensed the pleasant smile that crinkled the stranger's face was genuine. He felt some of his apprehension recede. The man stretched out a hand, and Peter responded in kind. His grip was gentle, but Peter sensed the stranger was a good deal stronger than his willowy build suggested.

"You've done a crackerjack job," continued the man as he released his hold on Peter's hand. Despite his unease, a smile flitted across Peter's mouth. It had been many years since he had heard that term.

"Thank you, but I haven't done all that much," said Peter. He took off his hat and ran the back of his hand across his forehead. He did this more to gain a few seconds to compose himself than to wipe away the sweat beading over his forehead. The stranger was friendly enough, but his abrupt appearance, seemingly out of nowhere, felt peculiar, mystifying. Peter couldn't entirely dismiss a continued sense of trepidation.

"I would say you've done a great deal," responded the man. "What inspired you to do all this?"

This question, being so terse and direct, further disconcerted Peter. He wasn't given to explaining what motivated him to do things, especially to someone he had never seen before. He shrugged almost imperceptibly and lowered his gaze to the ground. Rather than take this as a signal to drop the question, the man waited patiently for a response. When Peter glanced up at him, he saw that the stranger's eyes remained focused intently on him. His question appeared to hold great significance for him.

"Let's just say I wanted to do something for a fellow veteran," Peter answered reluctantly. The man stroked his plump beard. His eyes narrowed into slits, observing Peter's every move. Dumbfounded by such intense scrutiny from a total stranger, Peter once again lowered his head.

He looked up when he heard the man walking toward the broken headstone. Removing his hat, the man hovered over the stone, hands clasped together as though in prayer.

After several long moments, he placed his hat back on his head, looked over his shoulder, and uttered, "Thank you, Peter."

Despite the tenderness in the man's voice, as well as the warmth of the waning summer sun, Peter shivered as though ice water had been thrown in his face. "I don't believe we've ever met before," he stumbled. He tried to swallow but found he couldn't. "Have we?" he asked in a voice as dry as sand.

"No, we've never met until this moment," answered the man.

"Then how do you know my name?" demanded Peter, hoping the tremor in his voice wasn't as obvious as it seemed to him.

The man's benevolent smile gave Peter no hint of an answer. Without a word, he knelt down by the stone. He ran his fingers gently across the stone's broken edge with what appeared to Peter to be something akin to reverence.

Peter couldn't be sure whether five seconds or fifty had passed before the stranger stood back up. He moved with such little apparent effort that he appeared unencumbered by gravity. Rubbing the dirt from his hands, he pushed back his straw hat and gazed up at the sky.

As though on command, Peter also lifted his eyes heavenward. The sky was clear and vivid, made all the bluer by the white of the clouds and green of the trees. He searched the sky from horizon to horizon, trying to locate whatever it was the stranger saw. There was nothing special or unusual overhead. When he lowered his eyes, he saw that the man was once again studying him keenly.

"Once and for all, who are you?" demanded Peter. He tried to come across as strong and determined despite the shaking in his knees. Once again, the same inexplicable smile crossed the man's face. Had he noticed Peter's trembling knees? Was this a smile of sympathy or mockery?

"My name is Nathaniel Porter," he said.

Peter's mind blurred. He had a vague idea this name should mean something to him. As he tried to clear his head and focus his thoughts, his attention wandered over to the broken gravestone. His eyes widened. *The name on the gravestone!*

Suddenly frightened, Peter took a step back. "Why would you want to trick an old guy like me? Whatever the reason, you've had your fun. I'm sure you're happy with yourself." He picked up the pruning hook and, in his haste to get away, left the rest of Richard's tools behind.

"My regiment went up Marye's Heights," exclaimed Nathaniel Porter before Peter had taken two steps toward the cemetery gate, "with our shoulders bent against Rebel fire the way men walk into the teeth of a gale."

The words "Marye's Heights" unfurled like a battle flag across Peter's mind's eye. In a flash of recognition, he recalled the book on the Civil War he had been reading just a few hours earlier in the cottage. *Marye's Heights? This lunatic is referring to the Battle of Fredericksburg!* Peter was tempted for a moment to confront such a liar, whoever he was. Instead he took another quivering step toward the cemetery gate.

"It was something like that for the 16th, wasn't it?" asked Nathaniel. Peter stopped dead in his tracks. He stood frozen in place for a moment and then turned around slowly.

"What did you just say?" he asked, his head cocked to the side and his eyes aimed sharply at the man.

"Your regiment. Omaha Beach. June 6th—1944," the man said evenly. He paused, staring directly back into Peter's eyes with equal keenness; then he added, "Men dying all around you. Men screeching in pain and fear. Blood. Blood everywhere. As it was for me and my comrades at Marye's Heights."

Sweat streamed down Peter's face, and his shirt became soaked. He had never talked about his experience on Omaha Beach with anyone still living. How could this man possibly know about that terrible day with the 16th Infantry?

Peter's sight grew blurry, and his knees buckled. The man was at his side immediately. He gripped Peter's arms with his strong hands and gently helped him to sit down with his back against the iron fence. He hurried over to the jug Peter had brought with him. He poured water into a cup and brought it over to Peter, who took it and sipped gratefully. As soon as he drank the last drop, the man refilled it without being asked.

Somewhat revived by the water, Peter focused straight ahead. No one was there. He glanced to his right and was startled to see Nathaniel Porter, or whoever this was, squatting down alongside him.

"Why are you here?" whispered Peter, his voice raspy and flat.

"For the same reason you are."

"What reason is that?"

"To do what I can for a fellow soldier."

Peter shot him a questioning glance but said nothing. Instead he raised the cup back to his lips. It was empty. The man took the cup and filled it once again from the water jug. He handed the cup back and waited patiently while Peter drank from it.

"I'm Civil War; you're World War Two," continued the man after Peter had finished his third cup of water. "You and I both know how terrible war is. Only those who have been there can ever really know."

Peter looked the man straight in the eye, waiting for the slightest tremor or twitch to indicate the presence of deception. Not seeing even the slightest indication of duplicity in the man's countenance, he responded, "You're right. You have to have been there. Nobody can ever understand if they weren't there—Nathaniel."

The only sound was the wind gently blowing through the leaves around them. From the top of a nearby tree, a crow sang a melancholy series of lonely, grating caws.

"I haven't been sleeping well," Peter revealed. *Why, of all things to say, did those words come out of my mouth?* His voice sounded hollow to him, as though coming from deep within a cavernous well. He was even more astonished when he continued on in the same vein. But something told him if he were ever to speak about such matters, now was the time, and Nathaniel Porter was the person to tell them to. "I've been having strange dreams that wake me up. Nightmares. Last night was one. Maybe it was the storm. Big one, wasn't it?"

"I once enjoyed thunderstorms. When I was a child," said Nathaniel.

"So did I," answered Peter. "Just like you, when I was a kid. But that was a long time ago. Now thunderstorms make me think I'm right in the middle of battle again with shells exploding over and over, all around me."

Nathaniel considered this as he stared off at the trees over Peter's shoulder. "There was once a time when I had dreams like that."

Hearing this, Peter felt pulled by a current he was powerless to resist. He had no idea what this force was, where it came from or where it was taking him. Still, he went on. "It's always the same dream. I'm surrounded by dark, turbulent ocean water. I'm on a landing craft headed for a beach, but when the ramp finally lets down, I'm far out at sea, out of sight of land. The water's rough and choppy. I have to swim toward shore, but, all the while, I'm pulling a soldier I don't even know. He's crying and begging me not to let him die. In the dream, it makes my skin crawl to hear him."

He shut his eyes tightly to block out the sight and sound etched in his mind. "It does now, too," Peter added. He stopped, unable to say more.

"For you, it was a beach," said Nathaniel. "For me, a hill. But it's the same nightmare. The chaos of men shrieking in agony and fear all around you. The expressions of terror on the faces of your friends. The fountains of blood. The horror of brains and bowels spilling out all around you."

Peter cupped a hand over his eyes to block out what Nathaniel's words were bringing back to him. A moment passed. He felt

Nathaniel's strong hand on his forearm. Patiently, gently, as if Peter were a child, Nathaniel tugged his hand away. They peered into each other's eyes, eyes that had each seen battle. On a beach and on a hill.

"You and I are brothers-in-arms," said Nathaniel.

Peter wanted to believe this. But he couldn't. Not this. "No, not true, not true," he replied sorrowfully.

"Tell me why," said Nathaniel tenderly.

"If I tell you, you'll find out who I really am."

"Who are you really?" Nathaniel prodded gently.

Peter felt a sudden and irresistible impulse to run away. His heartbeat pounding in his ears, he struggled to get to his feet. As he did so, he caught a glimpse of Nathaniel's eyes drilling into his own. Peter froze, held in place by the authority of Nathaniel's kind expression. For a long minute, he said nothing, too afraid to speak.

"War doesn't end for a soldier when the last shot is fired," said Nathaniel mildly.

"No, it doesn't," responded Peter.

"Who are you really?" asked Nathaniel again, with the same tender softness.

Peter opened his mouth to speak, but no words came out. He closed his eyes, hoping that, when he reopened them, Nathaniel would have vanished as suddenly as he had appeared. Instead, with his eyes shut tight, he could feel Nathaniel's eyes scrutinizing him. Trembling, he bowed his head and clasped his hands in his lap as if he were seeking pardon.

"Who are you really?" asked Nathaniel a third time, his voice firm and commanding and yet filled with sympathy.

"I'm—a coward," replied Peter, surrendering to the unyielding power emanating from Nathaniel's presence. He wiped the back of his hand across his still-closed eyes to hide his shame. For this reason, he did not see Nathaniel's tight-lipped smile of respect. He untied the maroon kerchief from around his neck and handed it to Peter, who used it to swab his forehead and neck.

"What happened to you on June 6th?" asked Nathaniel with all the casual matter-of-factness of talking about a baseball game that had been played on that day.

Without hesitating a moment longer, Peter spoke the words he had kept hidden away for a half a century from everyone.

"The brass knew what it was going to be like. They put a bunch of green kids in the first waves because we didn't know what we were getting ourselves into. They knew that about us, alright. All wars are a betrayal of the young by the old." Peter's voice cracked. Nathaniel offered him more water, but he waved it off and continued.

"My best friend in those days was Tommy Hill. He was actually the best friend I've ever had in my whole life. We had been together since the train ride to basic training. That morning of June 6th, we went down the nets of the troopship side by side into the landing craft. I could see Tommy was frightened. I was frightened, too. We all were. But seeing the look on his face made me forget just a little that I was scared to death. I said to him, 'Nice day for a boat ride' or something foolish like that. Tommy tried to smile. I said, 'Stick with me, kid—we'll get through this.' The landing craft was bouncing around in the waves like a fishing bob with a bass on the line. We had been on board less than a minute when Tommy puked up all over me. I hollered at him, 'I told you to stick *with* me, not *on* me.'"

Peter chuckled in stark contrast to the grimness of his memory. "Poor guy could hardly stand up straight. I held him up as he kept apologizing. I told him it didn't matter. And it didn't. Here I was, covered down the front of my shirt with his breakfast, and it meant nothing to me. All that mattered to me was that he was my buddy."

Peter's voice trembled again, and Nathaniel lightly touched his arm for a moment.

"Tommy could hardly move. He shouldn't have been there. He was just a kid. So was I. All of us, just a bunch of scared kids. The landing craft stopped farther out than it was supposed to. We were so weighed down with equipment we could hardly move. I practically carried Tommy off when the ramp on our Higgins boat went down. The water was deeper than we had expected. As soon as Tommy and I stepped off, I went straight under. When I managed to swim back up to the surface, we were taking a hell of a lot of fire. Guys were getting hit and screaming all around me. I dog-paddled over to what I saw as the safety of a disabled tank that had taken a hit. I turned around and saw Tommy go under, come back up, and go under again.

"He was coughing and gasping. I thought, 'Go to him, get him!' But guys were pushing forward, trying to get out of the water and away from the bullets that were coming at us from the shore. We had been trained for months to move forward constantly, and every instinct in me told me not to fall back. But it wasn't training that kept me from going back to him. That's just the lie I've told myself for years."

Peter's voice broke. He put a fist to his mouth for a moment to keep more words from spilling out. He lowered his hand and forced himself to continue.

"I was afraid to come out from behind that tank and help my buddy when he needed me most. But then a voice inside me called out in my ear, 'Tommy's drowning!' Something inside snapped me out of it. Before I even knew what the hell I was doing, I started swimming back to him. He was less than 10 yards away. It took only a couple of seconds. Then, just at the moment I reached out to grab his hand, a bullet hit Tommy between the eyes and blew the top of his head off. He never knew what hit him."

Peter pressed Nathaniel's maroon kerchief tight against his face and kept it there for a long time before he spoke again.

"My whole damn life I've wondered what Tommy might have been if I hadn't hesitated those few seconds behind that stinking tank. A doctor? A teacher?

"All I know for sure is that it was my fault he died!"

For all of that time, he had feared the looks of disapproval and denunciation he was certain would follow if he ever confessed his hidden shame. But now, with that dreaded moment finally arrived, the only thing Peter saw in Nathaniel's kindly eyes was the last thing he would ever have expected: compassion.

"Only those of us who have been there know what it's like," repeated Nathaniel. "I tell you this: It wasn't your fault Tommy Hill died."

Upon hearing these words, Peter felt warmth coursing through his body, melting what had been cold and hard and unyielding in his heart. He felt soothed as an infant is soothed when held in his mother's arms.

And as when a child is comforted, he suddenly became sleepy. His eyes closed of their own accord, as if separate from him and beyond his control. His head tilted toward his chest.

"Thank you," said Peter, struggling to raise his head and look Nathaniel in the eyes.

"Why are you thanking me?" asked Nathaniel.

"For listening to me," replied Peter.

"As I have listened to you," declared Nathaniel with such forcefulness that Peter's eyes opened wide and he became fully attentive, "so must you listen as well."

"I will listen," agreed Peter without fully understanding what Nathaniel meant. But instead of asking, he said, "I wish there were something I could do for you."

"There is one thing."

"Anything," answered Peter as sleepiness returned, and his eyes once again began to close.

"Plant flowers here."

"Yes, I will do that," said Peter.

"Red chrysanthemums."

"My favorite flowers. How did you know? Tommy would like those, too," murmured Peter, on the edge of sleep.

"Tommy!" he cried out abruptly with his eyes remaining closed. "Tommy!"

CHAPTER THIRTEEN
The Things That Matter

J ENNIFER KNEW RICHARD rarely stayed in his boat
for more than a few hours when he went fishing.
This gave her hope that he might have returned while she was in
the cemetery with Peter. However, when the cove came into sight,
she was disappointed to see he was still fishing.

Her pang of disappointment quickly transformed into outright
resentment as she became convinced that Richard most likely
wouldn't be back until around sunset. She forced herself not to
take so much as another peek in his direction. *Why do anything to
exasperate myself even more?* The grumblings of a bad mood none-
theless intensified and overwhelmed her.

Trying to fight off a mounting discontent with her life in
general and Richard in particular, Jennifer threw herself into
straightening a pile of magazines, fluffing the pillows on the couch,
and throwing a few dishcloths and bath towels into the clothes
hamper. She hung some laundry on the clothesline to dry and then
swept every single pine needle and speck of dirt off the porch. All

to no avail. The harder she tried not to think about her husband, the more vivid the image off by himself on the lake became.

With a flick of her wrist, she tossed the broom across the porch and stormed inside, searching for some other task to attack. Last night's tableware in the dishrack next to the sink caught her eye. She flung the knives, forks, and spoons into the drawer under the spice rack. The dishes clattered together sharply as she piled them on top of one another.

She glanced at her watch as she plunked the glasses into the small storage cabinet by the refrigerator. Being so aggravated with Richard had made her temporarily forget about Peter back at the cemetery. Nearly three-quarters of an hour had passed.

He's just taking a little longer than he expected, she assured herself as she plopped down on the couch. *He'll be back in a minute.*

The minute passed. Then another.

The insistent little voice would not be silenced. *He's doing too much. It's still summer. The sun is so strong. He keeps himself in good shape, but after all, he's in his seventies. It's too hot for him to be doing all that work.*

She checked her watch again.

Why had she brought Peter that wine? She knew the answer at once. *Because I'm selfish. I was lonely by myself here in the cottage and put my own needs ahead of what was best for him.* Thanks to her, maybe he had grown tipsy from the second glass. Maybe he had fallen and hurt himself. Maybe he was lying on the ground right this second with blood flowing from a cut on his head! *And it's all my fault!*

The image of Peter bleeding and helpless because of her thoughtlessness was more than Jennifer could bear. She hurtled down the front steps and, in doing so, reaggravated her sore calf. Ignoring the sting in her leg, she limped toward the cemetery.

As she hurried as best as she could down the path, a long-ago memory of Heidi at the cottage materialized before her. Heidi had slipped on a submerged rock just a few feet out from the shore of the lake. She had walked up to the cottage, blood pouring down her face, and without so much as a whimper, walked inside and announced, "I've had a little accident." She couldn't have been more than five years old. Jennifer forced herself to hurry along even faster.

Just before the cemetery came into sight, Jennifer called out to Peter so as not to startle him. No response. Her fear growing by the second, she cried out again, louder this time. Once again, nothing. Her heart pounding with exertion, but even more from mounting fear, she ran the last few steps.

Reaching the cemetery, she was stunned to see her fear realized. There was Peter, sprawled out on the ground, eyes closed, back propped up against the cemetery's iron fence, his head tilted back, his mouth slightly agape.

She stared at him, frozen in place. He cried out suddenly. An icy sensation surged through Jennifer's body, and she shivered convulsively in the hot September sun. *Thank God he's alive! But what did he say? It sounded like he shouted a name.*

He shouted again. This time she heard distinctly. In an eerie, ghost-like voice, she had heard him call out, "Tommy!" She rushed over to him and knelt down by his side. She didn't know what to do. She brushed against his shoulder with just the tips of her fingers to wake him. No reply.

She grasped his shoulder firmly and shouted "Pop!" close to his ear. With that, he drew in a sharp breath and blinked several times. His eyes darted rapidly back and forth, searching for someone or something. Then, squinting, he stared vacantly as if not seeing her right in front of him. Was he tipsy from the wine? What are the signs of a stroke? Her mind flooded, unable to form so much as a single coherent thought. As she gaped at him, his eyes appeared to focus on her for a second.

"Jennifer, what are you doing here?" he mumbled, his words slurring into each other.

Should she run for help? Should she remain with him? Unable to think clearly, she felt as powerless to move as an animal snagged in a trap.

"You didn't come back when you said you would," she told him, not sure what else to do but answer his question. "I just came back to check on you."

"Check on me? That was very kind of you." He spoke slowly, his eyes trained on her. He began to sound a bit more like himself. Some of the tension eased from the muscles in her shoulders and neck. Maybe he was alright after all.

"Yes, I wanted to make sure you were okay," she said as she helped him sit up into a more comfortable position.

He cocked his head, peering at her with a questioning squint. "What would make you think I wasn't okay?"

"Well, I hadn't expected to find you lying on the ground like this. I thought for a second—" Her voice trailed off, leaving the sentence hanging in the air. She hurriedly changed the subject before he had a chance to ask what she had meant.

"I thought I heard you calling out a name as I approached you."

"A name?"

"Yes, I thought I heard you call out 'Tommy!'"

His eyes darkened, first in confusion and then in an angry scowl. "Were you spying on me?"

"Spying on you?" repeated Jennifer. She leaned away from him in astonishment. "Pop, are you sure you're okay?"

"I'm fine and dandy," he declared. "But you were listening in on my private conversation!"

"What are you talking about? There's nobody here but you and me."

"You were sticking your nose into something that is none of your damned business!"

Jennifer leapt to her feet as if Peter had pulled out a knife and pointed it at her. She drew her arms protectively across her chest and, bewildered, gaped at her father-in-law.

"I just wanted to be sure you were all set," she whispered meekly. Everything around her suddenly seemed enveloped in a panic-induced gauze.

"Oh, sure you did!" bellowed Peter. Jennifer spun around so he couldn't see her trembling. She fought against an overwhelming impulse to run out of the cemetery. With her back to him, she didn't see the anger in Peter's face melting into remorse second by second.

Jennifer wheeled around to face him. He was dismayed to see tears spilling down her cheeks. She made no effort to spare his feelings by wiping them away.

"I've wondered for years why Richard finds it so hard to be around you. I get it now."

Her hurt and pain conveyed to Peter the way electricity courses through a copper wire. He winced as though slapped across the face. It appeared that he, too, might burst into tears at any second.

"I'm sorry, Pop," she said, taking a tentative step toward him. "I shouldn't have said that."

Peter held his breath and bit down hard on his lip. When he exhaled through pursed lips, he made a sound like air escaping from a leaky tire valve.

"No, I'm the one who should apologize," he said. "I tend to act like a damn fool when it comes to my—privacy. I suppose you could ask Richard about that. I thought I was long past having my temper get the best of me when that happens. Obviously I'm not. I'm sorry I shouted at you."

Jennifer took another faltering step toward her father-in-law as he remained sprawled on the ground. She knelt down next to him and placed her hand on his shoulder. The harder she tried to think of something to say, the more contrived her words seemed to her. But if she said nothing, he would think she was still angry with him. Then, out of nowhere, she heard the very words she had kept to herself for so long. They sounded to her like someone else were speaking them.

"Why is it so difficult for us to talk to each other?"

He started to protest, but she knew what he was going to say and cut him off. Like a logjam breaking up when a single log is finally loosened, her words flowed out of her.

"I realize that, when we've visited you, I always tended to chatter away. I prattle on and on pretty much the entire time we were together. But that's not what I mean. Nobody in this family ever wants to talk with me about important things. Except Heidi." Her voice wavered. "But my daughter has her own life now. I can't depend on her to fill the empty space in my heart anymore. I never should have in the first place. It wasn't fair to her. She's just a kid."

Jennifer stopped, fearful she had already said more than her father-in-law wanted to hear. But when she snuck a peek in Peter's direction, she saw his eyes were riveted on her with such intensity she forgot what she wanted to say next. She lowered her gaze to the ground.

"You're right," said Peter. "We're not very good at talking to each other. Not about the things that matter. And I know I haven't been a good listener. There's no point in talking to someone who isn't listening. Is there?"

Jennifer felt Peter's eyes studying her every blink, every twitch of her eyebrows, every tremble in her lips. In the back of her mind, she heard a little voice laughing to think that, just when she was finally being listened to, she had no idea what to say. All she could do was nod in affirmation to his question.

"What do you want to talk about?" he asked.

She still could not raise her eyes to meet his. She didn't want tears. Not now. She made herself promise she wouldn't cry before she said another word. Believing the promise would be kept, she lifted up her eyes and said, "About when you called out Tommy's name a few minutes ago."

A moment passed, and he whispered, "Okay, I'm listening." She summoned up the courage to continue.

"A few moments ago was the first time I've heard you say Tommy's name in years. Richard has never talked to me about his brother. I tried to once. He got so upset that he stormed out of our apartment, pretty much the way he did last night."

Jennifer paused, not quite sure whether she should say more. When she glanced at him, his eyes told her to go ahead. "I know you miss your son," she said, this time without averting her eyes from him.

"I do. Every single day for almost a quarter of a century," replied Peter, his eyes darting back and forth as if he were watching a tennis match in his mind.

"What is it?"

"I don't want to give you the wrong impression," he said. "That's the same as lying, and I'm not going to do that. So—when you heard me, I wasn't calling out to who you thought I was."

"Who, then?" she asked.

"A friend of mine. Tommy Hill," he mumbled.

"Oh, I see," Jennifer said tentatively. "Would you tell me about your friend?" she asked. Her voice reminded Peter of the softness and warmth of a baby's blanket.

He remained quiet for so long that Jennifer became convinced he wasn't going to tell her anything more. She was about to give up yet again, get to her feet, and start back to the cottage when he at last broke the silence.

"He was my buddy during World War Two."

Jennifer leaned forward, her posture and expression telling him how much she wanted to hear more. Feeling powerless to keep his words from her for a moment longer, he acquiesced.

"Did they teach you about Omaha Beach when you were in school?" he asked. Her blank look told him she didn't know what he meant. "About D-Day? The Allied invasion of Europe? June 6, 1944?"

Jennifer nodded in recognition; then her face scrunched up in a puzzled expression. He answered her question before she could ask it. "Tommy and I were there that day."

Her jaw dropped, and she stared at him, open-mouthed. "Tell me," she blurted out as if asking him for the location of buried treasure.

He went to speak, but no words came out. He began again. Then again. Jennifer waited patiently all the while, allowing him as much time as he needed. She sensed it was not her place to help him find the words he was searching for. When he finally spoke, she was grateful she had remained silent.

"Tommy Hill was a good athlete. Fastest runner in the platoon during basic training. Excellent shot with a rifle, too. One of the best. A soldier's soldier." Peter hesitated a moment and then said, "And he was a good friend. Best friend I ever had."

When Peter didn't go on, thoughts flashed like lightning bolts through Jennifer's mind. Did she dare to ask another question? Where was the boundary for her father-in-law? What if he got angry again if she crossed it? But hasn't there been enough silence already? *Take a chance! What's the worst thing that could happen?*

"Could you tell me a story about the two of you?"

Jennifer again waited silently as she observed emotions of sorrow and amusement sweeping across her father-in-law's face.

"He had a girlfriend. He would show me her picture from time to time. Helen. Very pretty. Tommy liked to say Helen could melt an ice cube at the North Pole just by looking at it."

Jennifer laughed. Hearing her reaction, Peter did too. "He used to actually talk that way, believe it or not. He had plans to get married when we all got back to the States. Richard's mom and I married the day before I left for the army. It was fairly common for couples to do that before they shipped off overseas. Some of those marriages didn't make it when guys came back from the war, but Sarah and I were among the lucky ones. Our marriage made it. Anyway, Tommy and I used to talk about doing things together when we were back in civilian life. You know, go to the movies together on Saturday night with Sarah and Helen, Sunday dinners, picnics, all that sort of thing."

"Were you able to do that? Stay in touch with each other after the war?"

Peter's eyes clouded.

"Tommy was killed before we even got to the beach. Pretty much as soon as we disembarked from the landing craft," said Peter, his voice quivering. Jennifer took his hand and held it tight.

Over the years, Peter had gradually come to reminisce less and less about his friend and their time together in the war. Sometimes he would see two young couples walking down Main Street together, talking and laughing happily. Loneliness, sorrow, anger, guilt would then take turns tugging at his heart. He would try to distract himself by turning on the TV and watching a baseball game. Or he would do chores around the house, or work in the garden, weeding and watering his flowers. Anything to get his mind off Tommy Hill and the way the memory of his friend made him feel.

Now, with Jennifer's grasp on his hand like an anchor holding him in place, there was nothing Peter could do to escape those feelings. Without knowing it, she was preventing him from getting back to his feet so he could concentrate on raking away a few more leaves and twigs or pruning back another branch or two. His eyes watered. A tear ran down his cheek. Jennifer saw this and inched slightly closer to him, not letting go of his hand.

"I know you feel sad your friend died, Pop. It's okay to feel that way. Even after all this time," she said. He felt soothed once more by the gentle tone of her voice but couldn't speak. Not yet. He swallowed hard and kept his eyes focused on the ground.

"I never told you before about Tommy Hill, did I?" asked Peter after a minute or so had passed. Jennifer shook her head, confirming this. He tried to relax the muscles in his face by rubbing his hand vigorously across his mouth.

"I should have a long time ago," he continued.

"Why didn't you?"

"I guess it's because—" he began but then stopped. "The truth is I've been carrying around a boatload of guilt about my friend Tommy for a long time now."

Peter saw her mouth forming another question, and he cut her off. "There's no reason to go into the details." He turned slightly in the direction of the broken gravestone.

Though Jennifer was looking directly at him, she didn't notice his lips curling up into the hint of something like a smile or the all-but-imperceptible gesture he made with his eyes toward the stone. "It's enough to tell you I now realize something it took me a long time to find out. I don't have to blame myself anymore for what happened back then."

Jennifer heard a slight faltering in his voice. She sensed he had not yet completely convinced himself of the truth of his own words.

Questions called out to her, demanding answers. What did he blame himself for? Why had he carried a burden of guilt for so many years? What had he come to realize? When? How?

Then she heard another voice within her: *If he wants to tell you, he will.*

With that, her questions vanished like mist in the morning sun. Perhaps he would tell her someday. Perhaps not. The future would unfold as it would. But for now, she knew this wasn't the time for her to indulge her curiosity. It was enough to let this moment be what it was—no more, no less.

Once more, silence settled over them. Neither of them felt obliged to pass the time in small talk. They were pleased to just be together on a warm, late afternoon in September and feel an occasional cooling breeze waft over them. A minute or two passed by. Or maybe closer to ten or twelve.

"Pop, you know something?"

"What?"

Jennifer spoke slowly, measuring each word with care before speaking it. "You've been tending to the grave of an unknown soldier from the Civil War. You've been honoring—" She squinted at the writing on the stone. "—Nathaniel Porter. But I think you've also been honoring—"

Peter finished her thought before she could. "Tommy Hill," he said. He mulled this over. "I *am* the only one who knows how and where he died. Yeah, I guess you're right. Nathaniel Porter and Tommy Hill are both unknown soldiers in their own ways. And they each deserve to be honored."

"Pop—" Jennifer began again. She edged ever closer to him until their arms touched. Neither of them drew back from the other.

"Yes?"

"You've been an unknown soldier, too."

Peter recoiled as though sniffing a carton of spoiled milk. Jennifer braced herself for an angry retort. But instead of indignantly protesting, he quickly regained his composure and made himself consider what she had said. With a shy, sad smile, he let her know he'd heard her and had accepted the truth of what she was telling him.

"But you're not an unknown soldier anymore. Not to me."

Peter grimaced and shifted his weight. Jennifer wondered if his leg muscles had cramped up from sitting on the ground too long or if he just didn't want to talk about himself anymore. It didn't matter. She helped him rise to his feet.

As she did, a painful memory surged through her. She winced to recall the evening at Sunny Glen a few weeks ago with the beautiful young waitress who had so infatuated her husband. *What, of all things, would cause me to think about that?*

"So much of who we are remains hidden from us," she heard herself say as Peter steadied himself.

He cast a puzzled glance in her direction. "From me as much as anyone. Probably more than most," he said pensively after a moment.

Jennifer sensed he wanted to ask her something. She tilted her head and raised her eyebrows to assure Peter that she was prepared to listen intently to whatever he had to say.

"May I ask a little favor of you? Actually, maybe one that's not all that little," he added.

"Anything."

"I was asked to plant—" he began but then stopped. "That is, I'd like to plant some chrysanthemums here."

"Chrysanthemums!" repeated Jennifer. She again took hold of his hand. "That's a wonderful idea. And Hollister's Garden Market is open this holiday weekend. It's less than ten minutes away."

"I don't want to impose on you."

"You're not imposing on me. After all, it's the least we can do for an unknown soldier," she said as she pointed to the broken gravestone.

"Thank you, Jennifer," he said with his same shy smile. "I think we should go back to the cottage now."

He stepped forward. For a moment Jennifer thought he was going to hug her. Instead he reached down, picked up the rake and turned to walk away. They had taken only a dozen or so steps when Jennifer turned back. "We forgot the clippers," she called over her shoulder.

The clippers were close by—where she had first seen Peter lying on the ground. As she reached down to pick them up, she noticed a maroon bandanna. She picked it up and examined it. *Strange—I thought I gave him one of Richard's blue kerchiefs.* Knowing Peter was waiting for her, she shrugged, put the bandanna in her jeans pocket, and walked back to him.

"I hope they have red chrysanthemums," said Peter as he walked ahead of her on the narrow path.

"I have a feeling they will," she replied.

CHAPTER FOURTEEN

The Sight of Three
Baskets

I N THE HOUR OR SO it had taken for Richard's
boat to drift from the center of the cove to some
overhanging branches near the shore, he hadn't caught any fish other
than a few pumpkinseeds. He had thrown them back; it would be
better to return home with nothing than such embarrassingly puny
fish. He considered what might be causing his bad luck. *Maybe
the cold front that passed through last night?* Richard looked up at the
clouds dashing by overhead. He had caught fish in this location
before when it had been breezier. *Maybe it was the lure.*

After the second hour came and went, he reasoned that he
had spent too much time on the water to give up. It was the same
dilemma he had faced before. Quitting now could mean just missing
the catch that would justify all his patience. He rowed with sure
and efficient strokes back to the middle of the cove.

Another hour passed. Then another. He drank water from
the plastic jug he had brought and munched on granola bars. He
relieved himself into a portable urinal. And all the while, he knew
deep down that he was staying out on the water because his dad was

back at the cottage. With a shake of his head, he tried to dislodge an image of the two of them sitting down over a few beers and shooting the bull as he had heard fathers and sons sometimes do.

He tried forcing himself to deny that his father was the reason for his staying on the water. *I just want to bring back some fish for this evening's dinner.* Willing himself to believe the fish were due to bite any minute, he rowed to different spots in the cove to try his luck there. He cast and recast his line until the afternoon sun nudged the tops of the trees along the western horizon.

Finally, when the sun was shining through the leaves and its dappled light glittered over the water, Richard grudgingly accepted the inevitable. He reeled in his line and placed the fishing pole on the floor of the boat. He gripped hold of the oars and, turning the bow toward the cottage, rowed with long, deep strokes.

It felt good to exert himself after sitting for most of the day. He considered rowing out to the middle of the lake rather than heading straight back to the cottage. Richard was surprised by how strong he felt, as though he were in his twenties again. He swore he could row the entire circumference of this lake without tiring—just as he had done many times years ago.

He lifted the starboard oar out of the water and stroked a few more times with the portside oar. The boat swerved out toward the center of the lake. Then he lifted the portside oar and pulled hard to starboard. The boat changed course and headed back in the direction of the cottage. In less than a minute, he was once again back alongside the small aluminum dock Jerry Colville had installed years ago. Richard secured the boat, placed his pole, weather-beaten tackle box, and water jug on the dock, and then carefully stepped up from the boat.

He rubbed his hand along the length of his arm, pleased by the smooth bulge of his bicep under his long-sleeved shirt. He considered starting his old weight-lifting regimen in a few weeks after settling in for the school year. It had been several years since he had done any curls or bench presses, but he felt confident he could regain his old form in a month or so. For a few brief moments, he was the happiest he had been in more than a week.

The wind that had blown all day had finally died down. The air was now hushed and still. As he walked toward the cottage carrying the pole, tackle box, and water jug, Richard heard the sound of his father's voice. There was a pause, and Jennifer burst out in one of her loud, unrestrained fits of laughter. *Dad must have just told her one of his corny jokes.* He couldn't remember the last time he had heard that boisterous guffaw of hers. His smile vanished when he realized how much he missed hearing it.

Taking a few more steps, he detected the kitchen radio playing a song. Richard didn't recognize it at first but then caught the familiar strains of Creedence Clearwater Revival's "Lodi".

Nostalgia punched him in the gut with such force that he gasped. He stopped in his tracks and looked up at the soft, late-afternoon sky, waiting for this distressing surge of emotion to pass. Coming so soon after the pleasure he had felt a few moments ago, the pain was all the more difficult to bear.

He tried telling himself this was merely the same despondency he always felt at this time of year. Summer was coming to an end. It was time to head back to school. It had been this way ever since he had been a kid—then as a student, now as a teacher. But no, this was something more. Much more.

Struggling to compose himself, Richard considered the possibility that he had stayed out on the water too long and taken in too much sun. That seemed to make sense. *Why else should I be so moody? Too much sun can play tricks with your mind. Perhaps a little nap might be in order before it was time to eat.*

He hoped Jennifer wasn't counting on him to provide a sufficient catch of fish for dinner. *Too late now if she was.* But she couldn't say he hadn't tried. Neither could his father, for that matter. He forced a little smile to convince himself he was okay and then resumed trudging the rest of the way to the cottage.

The familiar aroma of steaks on the grill sizzling over charcoal briquettes greeted him as he reached the cottage steps. Jennifer had already taken care of dinner. *Good!* But at the same time, he was disappointed she had assumed he wouldn't catch enough fish to make a good dinner. His frustration over Jennifer's obvious lack of faith in him gave way to a sense of irritation with his life in general. But this was easier to deal with than the wistfulness of a moment before. *I'm so damn moody. I need to lie down.*

That burst of energy while rowing back to the cottage had depleted him. The cottage steps seemed suddenly as steep as a hillside as he climbed up them. He put his tackle box, fishing pole, and water jug in their accustomed place on the porch. Panting slightly as he turned to enter the kitchen, he noticed, in the growing darkness, something out of the corner of his eye by the door. He peered down and became puzzled by the sight of three baskets overflowing with red chrysanthemums.

Richard wiped his shoes on the front doormat and stepped inside the kitchen. The room became hushed the moment he entered it. Jennifer and Peter were seated at the table, shucking ears of corn for dinner. A third chair had been pulled back, an unspoken invitation for him to sit down and join them.

They glanced up at him. Richard turned his eyes away from their mingled expressions of hopeful anticipation and foreboding. He felt a lump growing in his throat. He knew they weren't sure whether to speak or even smile. They were afraid the least little thing might cause him to turn and run away. Again. For reasons they didn't understand.

His heart tugging him toward his father and wife, he reached out a hand toward the back of the chair. Just as he touched it, he pulled back as if the chair was a burning ember.

"I'm tired from being out in the sun and wind all day," he mumbled as he shuffled toward the bedroom. "Going to take a little nap before dinner." He opened the door and closed it quietly behind him.

After a moment, Peter and Jennifer returned to shucking the ears of corn. Neither spoke again as they finished their chore.

CHAPTER FIFTEEN
A Kinship of Sorts

THE EVENING MEAL passed mostly in silence until dessert was finished. Jennifer put down her fork after finishing the blueberry pie she had picked up at Hollister's and turned to Peter. "I wish it were the Fourth of July and not Labor Day. Then Heidi could have been here with us this weekend. She would've loved to see you."

"Yes, having Heidi here would have made it perfect," replied Peter. "But it's been wonderful being here with the two of you."

As though taking this as a signal, Richard rose abruptly from the table. He gathered up his plate, utensils, and glass, careful to balance everything before picking it all up. He took a few steps and paused halfway between the table and the sink; then he turned to face them. He moved so quickly his knife and fork fell clattering to the floor, where he let them remain.

"I behaved like a damned fool last night," he declared. "You know, when we were playing Scrabble."

"Well, nobody likes to lose, after all," said Jennifer after a moment of uncertainty on how best to respond. Both men noticed the anxious tremor in her voice.

"I suppose not," returned Richard. "Still, there's no excuse for acting the way I did. I just want you both to know I'm sorry."

Peter rubbed his chin for several seconds as he considered a prudent reply. "As they say, no harm, no foul." He looked up at his son and winked.

Richard acknowledged this conciliatory gesture with a quick nod. He brought his plate and glass to the sink. Then, with a little grunt, he turned around, stooped down to pick up the knife and fork, and placed them in the sink, too. He turned on the faucet, squirted in some liquid detergent, let the hot water fill the sink, and then strode back over to his easy chair. Nobody said a word the entire time.

Richard felt pleased with himself as he settled into his chair, having denied Jennifer any opportunity, after his father left tomorrow, to be unpleasant about last night's little scene. He picked up the teacher's edition of *The Story of America*, the text for the coming semester's honors history class, and sat back comfortably into his chair.

He read a few sentences and then raised his eyes cautiously from the book. Noticing how silent the room was and how motionless his father and wife were, he decided it wouldn't hurt to engage in a little conversation for a few minutes. He searched his mind for something uncontroversial to say. "I noticed there were some flowers on the deck," he said, suspecting he probably sounded a little too cheerful. "Are you planning to pretty up around the cottage?"

Peter and Jennifer glanced at each other to see who should reply. Jennifer cleared her throat. "Your father has been working on that little graveyard on the way to the lake."

"What little graveyard?"

"You know, that one with the iron fence Heidi used to play in. Remember? Just before the fork in the path that leads to Infinity," answered Jennifer.

"Oh, okay," Richard answered with a shrug. He resumed scanning the section on the Federalist Papers. He got only halfway through another paragraph before he looked back up.

"What did you do?" he asked, his tone just a bit less sunny than a moment ago.

"Not really all that much," answered Peter. "Just a little raking, pruning, tidying up, that sort of thing. I borrowed a few of your tools. Jennifer and I got those chrysanthemums to plant for one of the graves. I put everything back where they belong," he hastened to add.

Richard glanced over at Jennifer, his eyes asking her if he had heard correctly. Her tense, tight-lipped smile told him he had. He tried to refocus on James Madison, the Father of the Constitution, but to no avail.

"What made you decide to fix up an old, abandoned graveyard in the middle of the woods?" he asked, immediately annoyed with himself for asking. *Why can't I just keep my mouth shut?*

"I just think it's good to leave things better than the way you find them sometimes," answered Peter. Richard turned back to his textbook but looked back up before reading another sentence.

"It's not like anybody's going to see the work you did," said Richard, feeling powerless to stop himself. "Seems like a strange thing to do."

"I thought someone buried there deserved better," said Peter.

"Is this something you're in the habit of doing? Sprucing up neglected old graveyards?" continued Richard. *Don't ask questions! Just keep quiet!* But he felt powerless, like he was being swept along by a flooded river with no idea where he was headed.

"No, not at all. This was a first," said Peter, his eyes darting back and forth rapidly between Jennifer and Richard.

"What was so different about this particular graveyard?" replied Richard.

"Nothing—at first glance."

"'At first glance'?"

"Richard, for heaven's sakes," interrupted Jennifer, unable to keep silent another moment. "Your father did something really wonderful today."

"I'm sure he did."

"Well, then! You're quizzing him like he's one of your students," she said, failing to hide her aggravation with a half-hearted attempt at a light and airy tone.

Richard stared at her and then looked away when she didn't acquiesce by lowering her eyes as usual. He took off his glasses and rubbed his eyes.

"No, it's just that I can't imagine what would cause my father to spend an afternoon in a run-down old cemetery." He shrugged, put his glasses back on, and returned to his book, affecting a sudden air of nonchalance. "That's really all there is to it."

Several seconds passed again in silence. Squinting, Richard once again raised his eyes from the book. He appeared weary and confused. Ignoring a little voice that implored him to keep quiet, he demanded, "What *did* you notice—after your first glance?"

Peter studied his hands. They were trembling. *But why should that be? I'm just talking with my son. Well, there's your answer.* "I noticed one of the gravestones belonged to a Civil War veteran."

"That's the reason you decided to—tidy things up?" demanded Richard with a disapproving frown.

Peter straightened his back and breathed in deeply. "You could say that. I felt a kinship of sorts with him. I know that sounds odd, but—"

"Yeah—as a matter of fact, it does," sneered Richard.

"Are you forgetting your father is a veteran, too?" asked Jennifer, trying not to reveal the irritation that was mounting inside her with every word Richard spoke.

"No, of course not!" returned Richard indignantly.

Peter cleared his throat. "While I was raking leaves and pruning branches at the graveyard, things I haven't thought about for a long time came back to me."

Richard abruptly twisted around in his chair as though trying to dodge his father's words. With his back partly turned away from them, it appeared to Jennifer he was pretending they couldn't see him. "You big baby," she muttered under her breath.

She turned to Peter. "You must have so many stories of those days like the one you told me this afternoon."

"I suppose so," said Peter. "But it was a sad, terrible time."

Richard appeared to be reading his book, but he didn't see a word in front of him. *What in hell is going on here? All I did was ask about some damn flowers on the porch.* Now he felt a sense of foreboding, as if he were on the edge of a cliff. One false move, and he might tumble over into an abyss. Why should that be?

Richard's attempts at self-restraint suddenly crumpled. He sat up straight, whirled around in his chair, and eyeballed his father. "Now what are you talking about?" he demanded.

"The war," replied Peter.

"The war?" repeated Richard even more loudly.

"Richard!" Jennifer, close to her breaking point, cried out. "Don't yell at your father!"

Richard rubbed his left index finger and thumb across his eyes. He sat on the edge of his chair, his body like a coiled spring, liable to thrust forward at any second. Jennifer noticed a bead of sweat coursing down the side of his face.

"What war are you talking about?" asked Richard, straining to keep his voice under control.

"World War Two," answered Peter.

"The two of you spent the afternoon discussing World War Two? In a cemetery?"

"I told Jennifer about my friend, Tommy Hill," said Peter. He again straightened his back.

"Tommy Hill?" asked Richard.

"You never knew him. He was a friend of mine from my days in the army."

Jennifer noticed Richard's eyes widen for a moment before he rubbed his hand across his face. *Does he know that name?*

"I know this must seem odd to you," said Peter, not seeing the moment when Jennifer had observed Richard's startled reaction to the name "Tommy Hill." "I guess it does to me, too. But there was something very powerful about being in that cemetery today. It was as if the man buried there had been waiting for me. Maybe, in a sense, he was."

For a moment, Peter considered telling Jennifer and Richard everything about his experience with Nathaniel Porter. *My experience? Is that what it was? Or was it all a dream?* He glanced quickly at Richard and then at Jennifer. No—he would keep Nathaniel safe from suspicion, fear, and ridicule. Nathaniel, his brother-in-arms, would remain in his heart, known only to him until the day they joined each other in the place where men no longer go to war to die on hills and beaches far from home.

"I'm confused," said Jennifer.

"You're obviously not alone," snarled Richard under his breath.

"What's confusing you, Jennifer?" asked Peter.

She glanced at Peter, as if for support, and then turned toward Richard. "Did you know about Tommy Hill?" she asked. "Have you heard that name before?"

"I'm not answering any questions," said Richard. He folded his arms across his chest. *Just like a little boy holding his breath 'til he turns blue,* thought Jennifer. Despite her dim view of her husband at the moment, she spoke gently to him. "I'm just asking if you had ever heard of this friend of your father's."

"What's it to you?" Richard snapped.

"The look in your eyes when your father said his name," replied Jennifer, forcing herself to remain calm. "You seemed to recognize it."

Richard opened his mouth but said nothing. He waved away the thought with both hands. "What do you care?" he growled. "I'm not getting into this tonight."

With all the suddenness of a summer squall over the lake, Jennifer's temper swept away all her attempts to remain composed. She slapped her hands down forcefully on her thighs. Leaping to her feet, she paced back and forth in front of Richard. "Of course not! Maybe we can talk about this tomorrow? Or perhaps sometime next week? Next month? Next year?"

Richard's face hardened as a mirthless smile crept across his mouth. "Nice try," he said coldly, "but we're not getting started on this."

Jennifer held her head between her hands as though she had a sudden headache. "Why are there so many things I can't talk about with you?"

Richard leaned forward in his chair. He spoke very slowly, enunciating each word distinctly. "I am not going to discuss anything having to do with my father spending the afternoon in an abandoned cemetery."

He paused, trying to gather himself as best as he could. "And I sure as hell am not going to talk about a man I never met. Some 'Tommy Hill.'" He stared back and forth at them, daring either to say another word.

"You don't get to decide for all of us, Richard. Not anymore," replied Jennifer, surprising not only Richard but herself with this unexpected show of dissent. Surprise hardened into resolve, and she went on. "It's always been this way. Our entire marriage. I've never understood why. And now, it's gotten to where we can't even discuss your father's friend who died fifty years ago. Why are there all these secrets?"

Peter turned to Richard, who continued to sit facing away from them. "I'm not a young man anymore. I don't know when I'll see the two of you again. Who knows, at my age, maybe—"

"Damn it! I'm not a child!" Richard said brusquely, interrupting his father. "Don't try to manipulate me!"

"What your father is saying is true," said Jennifer, as she sat back down on the edge of the couch. "None of us is going to live forever. Who knows what the future holds? Now is the time to talk!"

Richard wheeled around to face her. "Can't you be on my side just for once?"

"Richard, I'm always on your side," Jennifer said, unable to conceal how much his words had hurt her. Peter grew indignant when he saw the look on her face but managed to hold his tongue.

"Prove it and be quiet!" His burst of anger pushed Jennifer back against the couch like he had struck her with his fist. She curled herself up tightly into a protective ball, wincing as she did so from the still-tender cut on her calf. Peter bit his lip.

Richard raised himself stiffly to his feet. He stomped over to the refrigerator, flung open the door, and grabbed a pitcher of water. He took a glass from the cabinet over the kitchen counter and poured it half full.

Peter trained his attention on his son's every move, waiting for his own anger to subside before he said anything. Richard, keeping his back to them like there was no one else in the room, took long, slow sips of water.

From far off, a distant rumble of yet another storm penetrated the still, muggy air. Peter shuddered as the thunder grew louder and more insistent. His apprehension over the storm's approach made him forget how cross he had been with his son only a few moments before. "Jennifer's right. The time has come to tell the truth," Peter said. Neither Richard nor Jennifer gave any indication they had heard him.

"Tommy Hill was a friend of mine in the Army," Peter went on as if they had asked him to continue. "We landed on Omaha Beach together on D-Day. He was killed that day. I've never forgiven myself for not saving him."

Richard's hand halted as he brought the glass up to his mouth. Another roll of thunder echoed across the lake. The storm was closing in on them fast.

"I loved Tommy like a brother," said Peter, forcing himself to press on as fear and grief constricted his throat. "At the end of that terrible day, I bivouacked under a tree just beyond the beach. I made a promise to Tommy then and there, before I fell into a fitful sleep, that if I ever had children, I would name my firstborn son after him."

The glass slipped out of Richard's hand and crashed into the sink, shattering. Jennifer jumped up from the sofa and bounded awkwardly toward him. She put her arm around his shoulder. "Richard, are you alright?" she asked.

Richard shrugged his shoulder to dislodge her arm. He turned and stepped away from her. "No, goddamn it," he exclaimed. "I am not alright."

He turned toward his father, his face a mask of torment.

"Why are you digging all this up?" he demanded. "Leave it in the past, where it belongs. Let everybody just rest in peace." He summoned up the will to shout, "Especially my brother!"

Peter pushed himself up off the couch. He glared at Richard and shouted, "No more lies! No more hiding from the truth!" He closed his eyes and took a deep breath. When he spoke again, he did so slowly and deliberately. "Your brother is at peace, Richard. But you and I aren't. We haven't been for many years. I've never understood why. The time has come to face that fact head on."

Richard trudged over to his chair and collapsed heavily into it. He bowed his head and covered his eyes with his right hand. Jennifer sat back down on the edge of the couch across from him. Peter wobbled for a moment as he lowered himself back onto the couch next to her. Lightning flashed through the storm-darkened room, followed a few seconds later by another rumble of thunder.

"Richard, you and I have never talked about your brother," began Jennifer.

"Stop!" commanded Richard. "None of this would be happening if it wasn't for *you*, Jennifer!"

Jennifer paused for a moment to consider this; then she resumed, surprised by how even and under control her voice sounded to her. "I tried to once, when we were first married. Do you remember?"

She waited for a response, but he said nothing, his face shielded by his hand. "You stormed out of the house," she continued matter-of-factly, "and didn't come home until the next morning." Jennifer paused again, waiting for Richard to say he remembered. To say anything. He remained silent, so she went on.

"Even though I found out early on I couldn't talk about him, I've often thought about Tommy through the years. It's always been bittersweet knowing there was once someone who looked just like you."

"Looked alike, talked alike, walked alike," mused Peter. "If one wore the other's hat, I'd get them confused every time." He forced a sad little chuckle. "Identical twins," he added.

"My brother-in-law," said Jennifer. She thought this over. "I wish—" Her voice broke, and she couldn't go on.

Peter waited for her to regain her composure. "What do you wish, Jennifer?" he asked gently.

She could hardly be heard over a gust of wind beating against the side of the cottage. "I wish I could have seen Tommy and Richard together."

"Well, you never will!" shouted Richard. "And all the wishing in the world isn't going to change that. I want this conversation to stop!"

"Sons learn from their fathers," said Peter, ignoring Richard's command. "I always kept everything bottled up inside me. That's how I thought real men handled things. And I forced everyone else to do the same. Especially you. I've come to see that."

"Look, nobody is blaming you for what happened in the past," said Richard. He made his best effort to speak calmly, but his words still rose in pitch and intensity as he went on. "But this is my house, Dad, and I don't want to talk about this subject here. Especially not here!" He pounded his fist on the armrest of his chair with each of those three last words.

Peter stared helplessly at Richard. Having no idea what to say next to this man who was more a stranger to him than a son, he turned to Jennifer.

"After my Tommy died—" began Peter. He paused to compose himself. Lightning flashed in the distance, followed a few seconds later by an accompanying peal of thunder. "I was afraid that if I started to cry, I'd never be able to stop."

Lightning illuminated the trees for an instant like the gleam from an enormous camera bulb.

"The time for grief has passed," replied Richard, unmoved by the emotion in his father's voice. "We put that away a long time ago." Thunder resounded again, ever closer. "And now we need to let it be."

Peter started to speak but was cowed into silence as lightning lit up the room, followed by an immediate crack of thunder. Seeing Peter jump in terror at the sound, Jennifer stretched out her hand to him. He took it in his and squeezed hard, but she didn't draw back or wince in pain. "Don't you see?" she asked, turning to Richard. "You never really did put the past away. And we'll never be at peace until—"

Richard leapt to his feet as though twenty years old again.

"Until when, Jennifer?" he demanded, hovering over them both. "Until we all sit around and bawl our eyes out? How long for that? All night? 'Til next week? The rest of our lives?"

Lightning illuminated the room, followed immediately by a cannonade of thunder. Like a runner responding to a starting gun, Richard spun round and charged toward the door.

Unable to comprehend what was happening for a moment, Jennifer sat where she was until Richard reached the door and put his hand on the doorknob. She sprang to her feet. "No, Richard! Don't run away from us! Not again!" begged Jennifer as lightning flashed and thunder reverberated simultaneously.

Richard pressed all his weight against the door. With his hand still on the doorknob, he turned to face them. "I've been running away for twenty-four years," he declared with eerie indifference. "Why stop now?" He appeared for a moment to be searching for an answer to his own question, but, not finding one, he nudged the door a crack.

"Richard, talk to us about this," begged Jennifer. "Whatever it is. No matter what. Please talk to us."

Opening the door wider, Richard took a step away from her and shook his head emphatically.

Peter got up and walked up behind Jennifer. He lightly touched her shoulder to either support her or to steady himself. "You can tell me, son."

"No—I can't tell you," Richard replied.

"That's not true. I know I didn't always listen to you in the past, but I'll listen now. I promise," said Peter.

Richard stepped out onto the porch. "If I tell you, you'll hate me."

Just then, there was an ear-piercing crack as lightning hit a nearby tree! All three of them jumped. Peter cried out in terror and covered his head with his arms. Richard instinctively took a step toward his father but then quickly turned, bounded down the porch steps, and ran out into the pouring rain.

Jennifer limped after him for a few steps, but Richard was already in his car. The car's engine started, and the lights flicked on. She turned back to Peter. His arms were still raised over his head. His knees were shaking so much she feared he might fall. She hurried over to him and held him as tightly as she could.

CHAPTER SIXTEEN

Two Cups of Chamomile Tea

T HE SECOND STORM in as many nights had passed
more quickly than the first. Rain had fallen
in torrents, but for no more than several minutes, and soon the
thunder and lightning were fading away in the distance. The chill
air coming in behind the storm's wake made it feel like October
had pushed aside September without any warning.

Jennifer took one of her sweaters from a hanger in her closet
and got one of Richard's sweatshirts from the bureau for Peter.
Even dressed warmly, they still shivered from the rapid dip in
temperature. She decided to make a fire in the fireplace.

Crinkling up the sports section of a newspaper from last April,
she threw a handful of twigs on top of the paper, then strategically
placed small branches over them. Soon there was a crackling blaze,
and the room filled with the sweet fragrance of burning maple.
After a few minutes, she put on leather gloves and carefully posi-
tioned several larger logs over the branches.

Satisfied the firewood was fully ablaze, Jennifer asked Peter if
he would like a cup of tea. He said he would, and she went to the

kitchen. When the water was whistling in the teapot, she poured the water into two powder-blue mugs, each holding a bag of her beloved chamomile tea. She brought the cups over to the couch, handing one to Peter. He accepted it with a wan smile but said nothing.

She sat down on the side of the couch near the chair where Peter was sitting. Together they regarded the gleaming light and listened to the crackling of the burning wood. After a few minutes sitting in the comforting silence, Jennifer took out her knitting needles and a skein of burgundy yarn to work on the sweater she was making as a Christmas present for Heidi.

"Keep in mind, this isn't the first time this has happened," she said as she began working on the sweater.

"What's that?" answered Peter.

"The first time Richard has run out of the house the way he did this evening."

"He's always had an impetuous nature." agreed Peter. He was quiet for a minute and then added, "You'd think he would have outgrown such a tendency, but I guess it's like he said last night: some things never change."

Jennifer nodded and resumed knitting the sweater for Heidi where she had left off. Seeing this, Peter thumbed through Richard's collection of magazines in the rack by his chair. He found a fishing magazine, but before he opened it, he moved his chair so that its arm touched the arm of the couch. And so they sat side by side, she knitting and he gazing into the fire after the magazine held no further interest for him.

The tea warmed Jennifer on the inside as the cheerful fire did outwardly. And knitting, as it always did, calmed her and helped her to center. As the minutes passed, a sense of comfort settled over her like a warm cashmere blanket.

Soothed by the blaze and the chamomile tea and focused on the sweater, Jennifer had half-forgotten Peter was sitting beside her, so she was startled when he said, "This reminds me of waiting up for Tommy and Richie when they were teenagers."

"Parents never stop worrying about their kids, do they?" she asked, putting her hand up to her mouth to stifle a sudden yawn.

Peter didn't say anything in response, and this immediately made Jennifer anxious. Should she explain that she had yawned because she was tired, not because she didn't care about what he had said? Maybe she shouldn't have had the cup of chamomile tea after all, no matter how much it relaxed her. It always made her so sleepy, and now it was all she could do to keep her eyes open. It wasn't like Peter visited every weekend. What had she been thinking?

"It's a lifelong occupation," he said at last.

Jennifer was relieved to see a little smile cross his face as he said this.

She had knitted for so many years that she could carry on a conversation or watch a movie on TV without dropping a stitch. She sometimes wondered if she could knit in her sleep; now it seemed to her she might actually find out. Peter had noticed how she'd jumped when he broke into the silence before, so this time, noticing her drooping eyelids, he cleared his throat before saying, "That's going to be a fine sweater when you're finished with it."

"Sorry," Jennifer apologized after yawning again. "It's for Heidi. I've made so many sweaters for her; she'll probably just give it to her roommate. By the time she graduates, every girl on her dorm floor will have a sweater I knit for her."

She put the back of her hand to her mouth to stifle a prodigious yawn. "Oh, my. I'm sorry!" she said. "It gets dark so early now; it seems later than it actually is."

Trying to keep yet another yawn at bay, she returned to knitting as if Heidi would freeze to death her first winter at Fillmore College without it. After several minutes, she put her knitting needles down.

"Could I ask you a question?" she asked tentatively.

"Of course! Ask me anything on your mind," responded Peter.

"You called Richard 'Richie' a minute ago," she said, putting her knitting needles down. "I don't remember you ever calling him that before."

Peter mulled this over. He started to speak, but, as soon as he did, a yawn of his own escaped him. "Guess I'm catching whatever you've got." They both chuckled. "Did I? Probably haven't called him 'Richie' since he was in college."

"Maybe it's because you're remembering back to the time when 'Richie' was the name you used most often," offered Jennifer, saying the first thing that came to keep her alert. She stretched her eyelids as wide as she could to keep them from closing.

His lower lip jutting forward, Peter considered this for a moment. "I haven't thought about those days for a long time. Strange." He pondered further. "But not as strange as what Richard said."

"About you hating him?"

"Nothing could cause me to hate him," said Peter emphatically, despite his own increasing weariness.

"I know," replied Jennifer.

Peter rubbed his chin. "When the boys were little," he said, "I'd tuck their little pumpkin heads into bed, give them a kiss on their foreheads and tell them both, 'Daddy loves you very much.' I thought a father was supposed to stop that kind of talk as his sons grew older. That was foolish of me. Now it's too late."

Peter's words roused her out of the state halfway between sleep and wakefulness. "Never too late," she said, not entirely sure what she meant by that.

"Maybe," replied Peter, staring into the fire. Considering how the weekend had gone thus far, he doubted that Richard would be receptive to hearing anything, especially expressions of affection, from him.

He turned to ask Jennifer what she thought about this trait in men. She had fallen asleep. He thought about waking her up. *No, let her sleep. It's good just having her close by.* He reached up to turn off the floor lamp by his chair. He turned back to the fire, now the only source of light in the room, and contemplated the orange-yellow glow of the embers. In a matter of seconds, his head tilted forward, and he, too, was fast asleep.

CHAPTER SEVENTEEN
One Snowy Winter Day

W HEN RICHARD CAME TO the curve in the dirt road leading to the cottage, he turned off the truck's headlights. After all these years, he knew every rut, crevice, and stone in the road. Now that the storm had passed, there was just enough light from the waxing gibbous moon for him to see the road bordered by the underbrush on either side. He drove slowly, not so much to avoid a tree or large rock, but to keep his approach undetected by his wife and his father.

Richard stopped the truck several dozen feet from the usual place where he parked and turned off the engine. He waited a minute to see if anyone would notice he had driven up. He breathed a sigh of relief when nobody came to the window. Still, he waited a few more minutes to be certain they had gone to sleep.

Reasoning that he couldn't wait outside all night, Richard got out of the truck, eased the door shut, and snuck up to the cottage. When he reached the steps, he considered taking off his shoes but decided that wouldn't be necessary. He knew they wouldn't squeak as he went up them. Sure enough, he ascended noiselessly.

He couldn't dismiss the surge of pride he felt when he remembered Jennifer telling his father that he had built such sturdy, long-lasting steps himself. Placing his hand gently on the doorknob, he slowly twisted it and entered.

Just as he had hoped, his father and wife were asleep. The fire had burned down to a few lingering yellow embers.

Richard felt chill air rush past him as he opened the door. He tiptoed over to the cedar chest, lifted the lid, and took out a quilt. Holding it up close to his face, he breathed in the faint scent of red cedar. It was the quilt Jennifer had created the first year they were married. As if she were not in the same room with him, a wave of longing for her swept over him.

As Richard stared at the dim figures on the couch and the chair in the flickering glow from the remaining cinders, he realized he had a dilemma. There was only one quilt. He stood fixed in place for a moment; then he went to his father, bent forward, and gently covered him.

Turning around, Richard stepped toward the bedroom to take a blanket from the bed to cover Jennifer. Just as he reached the bedroom door, he was stopped in his tracks by his father's voice softly calling out to him.

"Thank you, Richard."

Jennifer stirred when she heard Peter's voice. She reached up and clicked on the three-way bulb to its lowest setting. In the lamplight, Richard saw his father smiling sleepily at him. He gave an anxious half-smile in return and then hurried to the bedroom to fetch the blanket for Jennifer. He returned and covered her with it in the same gentle manner as he had his father. She smiled at him with sleepy eyes, and he shyly smiled back.

"It's been quite a while since I waited up for you to come home," whispered Peter.

"I didn't bang up the truck, so that means you won't have to take away my keys," replied Richard.

Peter, not expecting a joke, stared at Richard for a moment with a puzzled expression. His face lit up suddenly in recognition. "I won't have to ground you, after all," he joked in return.

"Thanks. It would be tough getting around without my truck," replied Richard, annoyed with himself for his nervous giggle.

"Yes, that would be an inconvenience," said Peter in a serious tone, as though this were a real possibility.

Richard shivered and wrapped his arms tightly across his chest. "I should be grounded," he said before Peter could ask if he wanted the quilt. "I've been way out of line. You and Mom didn't raise me and—" He paused. "—raise me that way." He stared down at the floor for a second but immediately raised his eyes back to his father.

Peter acknowledged Richard's apology with a wave of his hand.

"I know you're upset with me, too," said Richard, turning to Jennifer. "I don't blame you a bit. I've been acting like a damn fool."

"If you don't mind a little fatherly advice," Peter offered cautiously, "the two of you might want to take a little walk to a special place after I leave tomorrow. There's such a lovely view of the lake."

"Infinity," replied Richard, glancing back over at Jennifer. "One of your favorite places in the world. That's a good idea." He waved goodnight to his father and turned to go to bed.

"Richard?" ventured Peter hesitantly as Richard opened the bedroom door.

"Yes, what is it?" asked Richard with a trace of impatience.

"I just want to say—I want to tell you—" He paused to clear his throat. "I want you to know that I could never hate you."

"I know, Dad," replied Richard from over his shoulder. "Like I said, I've been behaving like a damn fool." He turned back to the door, one hand on the doorknob.

"Nothing could ever make me hate you, Richard."

"I realize that," sighed Richard. He suddenly felt lightheaded and gripped the knob tightly to steady himself. He felt a wave of fear pass through him. *Am I having a heart attack? No, I've just exerted myself too much when rowing. I'm okay.*

"I've been sitting in this chair all evening wondering why my son would say such a thing."

"It was nothing, really. Let's just forget it."

"Not an easy thing to forget," said Peter.

"I understand that. And you're right. But there's no point in bringing it up again."

"I can't have you thinking for even a second I could ever hate you."

Richard took a deep breath to keep his rising testiness under control. "I know—you've already told me. I know you don't hate me."

"We both miss Tommy," said Peter. Richard loosened his grip on the doorknob as if his hand had suddenly lost all its strength. "But—I miss you, too," added Peter huskily.

Jennifer put her hand to her mouth, but too late to hold back a whimper.

"Don't do this—" whispered Richard, leaning against the door. "If you only knew—"

"If I only knew what?"

"If you only knew me," mumbled Richard.

"You're my son!" objected Peter. "Of course, I know you!"

"There are things about me you don't know," muttered Richard.

"I don't know *everything* about you, not all the details of your life," replied Peter. "After all, we've hardly seen each other for years.

It pains me to think of how many. Still, I know your character. I know you're a good man."

Richard grimaced. He shook his head vehemently to let his father know that he in no way considered himself to be a good man.

"You *are* a good man!" protested Peter. "What would ever make you think you're not?"

Richard again shook his head. "Let's just get some sleep."

"Get some sleep!" exclaimed Peter, frustration welling up in his voice. "First you tell me I could hate you. Now you tell me you don't think you're a good man." Peter held up his hands in despair. "How can you expect me to 'get some sleep' after saying such things to me?"

His brow deeply furrowed, Richard appeared to be deliberating over how to answer the question posed to him by his father. He stared at the pitch-black darkness outside the window; then he turned to directly face his father.

"You think you know who I am?" challenged Richard. "Maybe you don't."

Before Peter could say anything in response, Richard continued, "Do you remember how strict you were about me—about Tommy and me—staying out of your stuff? How angry you'd get if we messed around with the papers in your desk?"

Peter stared open-mouthed in response to Richard's question. He raised his hands once more and then helplessly dropped them to his sides. "I don't remember specifically," he said. Rubbing the fingers of his right hand across his forehead, he appeared to be trying to draw up a long-buried memory that would answer his son's bizarre question. "I'm sure I was overly strict about such things." He paused. "Has it been my sternness in those days that's been troubling you all these years?"

"A good man is first a good son. And it only stands to reason that a good son wouldn't disobey his father," answered Richard. "Especially when it had always been perfectly clear that nosing around in your stuff was a violation of the rules. Right?"

Peter glanced at Jennifer, wordlessly pleading with her to help him understand. She had no more idea why her husband was saying all this than Peter did. She brushed away a tear trickling down her cheek and forced herself to resume listening. There was nothing else she could do.

"Richie, isn't that a small thing after all these years?" asked Peter as he turned back toward his son. "All that was such a long time ago. Don't fret over such things. I was wrong to be so strict with you, and I'm sorry. But what does that have to do with here and now?"

Richard grasped the back of a dining-room chair to steady himself. "What did you just call me?" he asked plaintively.

Peter stared back at him with a blank expression.

"Your father called you 'Richie,'" said Jennifer quietly. She silently cursed herself for saying even this. *For God's sake, just be quiet*, she told herself.

A memory came to Richard. One time, when he was a teenager, he had gone to the Rhode Island shore with a group of friends. Swimming in rough surf, he had been caught in a rip current. His friends had rescued him from the grip of the offshore flow by pulling him parallel to the shore. He now felt the same sense of being dragged against his will by a power greater than his own.

In an attempt to gain at least a façade of control, Richard turned to Jennifer with a scowl. "Are you happy now? This is what you've wanted ever since we got here, isn't it?"

She didn't reply as Richard glowered at her. He turned back to Peter. "Okay, let me tell you something about 'Richie'—and the Tommy that you didn't know." He interlaced his fingers and cracked his knuckles. Jennifer shuddered at the sound, as Richard knew she would.

"When we were kids, the two of us used to sneak into your stuff," Richard murmured. Peter's eyes widened in anger for a second, but he managed to keep his mouth clamped shut.

Seeing this reaction, Richard swallowed hard and forced himself to go on. "One time, we found some old letters of yours hidden in a shoebox in the bottom drawer of your dresser. They were letters you had written to Mom when you were overseas fighting in Europe. We snuck them up to the attic with us and read them one snowy winter day when school got canceled."

"Why would you have done such a thing?" shouted Peter, the force of his words piercing the still night air. Jennifer wrapped her arms around herself protectively and shuddered again. Peter caught her reaction out of the corner of his eye and shielded his face with his right hand.

In that moment, he heard Nathaniel's voice whispering to him as surely as though the young soldier were in the room with him: "As I have listened to you, so must you listen as well." Peter lowered his hands from his face, determined to listen to every word Richard had to say, without another word of interruption escaping from his mouth.

"Because we were kids! Why else?" said Richard, biting off each word. He tilted his head, and his eyes narrowed in thought as he considered his own words. "No, that's actually not the reason," he said in his abruptly pensive state of mind. "We weren't just being mischievous and sneaky for the fun of it. That's not who we were."

He once again swallowed hard and continued. "Earlier today you probably got the impression I didn't know who Tommy Hill was. But that was an act. My brother and I knew all about him being your friend in the war from reading your letters. Neither of us dared to breathe a word about him. We feared you losing your temper with us, because we knew you wouldn't stand for us invading your privacy. And we were right to be afraid. Weren't we?"

With a reluctant nod, Peter acknowledged what his son was telling him.

"Do you really want to know why we were sneaking around?" asked Richard, momentarily flustered that his father had acquiesced so quickly. "Because we wanted to know who you were," he continued. "And that was the only way we knew how to find out. And I'll tell you something else. When we found out who you were, we were proud, damned proud, that our father had been at Omaha Beach on D-Day. Tommy and I would read all about D-Day in library books and say to each other, 'Dad was there.'"

A faint, rueful smile crossed Peter's face like a sunbeam peeking from behind a cloud. Just as quickly, his smile vanished.

Richard suddenly felt very tired. *I used up too much energy being out on the lake all day. And now this.* He trudged over to the sink. Placing his hands heavily on the lip of the porcelain basin, he stared out the window at his reflection.

"We practiced saluting each other up there in the attic," he continued, more to himself than to his father and wife. "We tried to imagine how you had once saluted. We actually got pretty good at it by pretending we were saluting you."

Remaining fixated on his reflection in the window above the sink, Richard fell silent.

"I don't know what to say," whispered Peter after making sure Richard had nothing more to say at the moment. "I didn't know any of this."

Peter ran his fingertips across his forehead in a circular pattern. Jennifer wondered if she should ask him if he wanted an aspirin. *No, be quiet.*

"I'm glad to know my boys were proud of me," said Peter. He pressed his hand across his mouth to keep from speaking further until he gathered himself. "Listen to me, son. Those letters didn't reveal everything. They weren't the whole story. Far from it. I didn't want your mother to worry. I kept things from her. I didn't tell her all there was to tell. My letters didn't reveal all of who I was back then. All that was happening to me. There were things I left out, things I've never told a living soul." *At least until today.*

"But you were proud of what you were doing. You were fighting 'the good war,' answering your country's call," said Richard, still staring out the window.

"People who like to talk," said Peter with an edge of contempt, "about 'the good war' have never known what it is to have bullets whizzing around their heads. Ricocheting off metal all around them. Thudding into the bodies of their friends. Anybody who calls war 'good' doesn't know a damn thing he's talking about."

Jennifer drew her legs up to her chest. The pain from the still-tender gash on her calf made her wince. She rocked back and forth, trying to calm herself the way she had once rocked Heidi to sleep when she was a crying baby.

"Richard, I'm trying my best to listen to you," said Peter, "but I don't understand what you're getting at."

"Never mind," said Richard, growing ever more tired.

"Now's the time to get it all out in the open," implored Peter. "I'll be going back home tomorrow. Who knows when we'll get another chance to finally understand each other? Or if we *ever* will?"

"I'm too tired. Just forget all this, okay?" said Richard. He pushed his hands down against the top of the sink to steady himself.

"Forget?" cried Peter. "I don't want to forget. Tell me everything you remember. All of it!"

"Remember all of it?" exclaimed Richard. He turned away from his reflection in the window to face his father. A moment before, Richard had strained just to keep his eyes open. Now, as a surge of adrenaline coursed through his body, his face flushed, and he breathed as hard as though he had just rowed across the lake again. "You want to remember all of it?" he repeated, taking a step forward.

Keeping his eyes locked on Richard's face, Peter nodded and replied, "I'm listening."

"Okay, then. Let's remember one of your sons, the one with the starched and pressed uniform, the polished shoes, the clean-shaven son with the buzz cut. That son looked like you at the same age, right down to the sergeant's stripes on the sleeves."

Richard paused to catch his breath and then resumed with renewed intensity.

"But you had another son. He looked exactly like the first son, except for a few minor details. Scruffy hair down to his shoulders. An unkempt beard. Tie-dyed shirt, beads, and ripped jeans. That was the son who marched down Main Street in front of your old Army buddies sitting on the front porch at the Army-Navy Club, chanting, 'Hey, hey, LBJ, how many kids did you kill today?'"

Richard let those words sink in. "Do you remember that son? That was me!" Richard divulged, thumping his chest so hard with his fist with each word that he winced in pain.

"Lots of kids dressed like that back then," Peter reasoned, his voice little more than a hoarse whisper.

Richard took another step toward his father, but Peter's gaze still didn't waver an inch. "But not all kids, right? A few like

Tommy put on uniforms and went to Vietnam and fought for their country. Guys like me thought guys like Tommy were crazy. But Tommy was a throwback to your generation. He read all those letters from you to Mom when you were off fighting the Nazis, and he never once forgot how proud he was of you. You were his hero. He wanted to be like you," said Richard. He paused and wiped roughly at his eyes. "Come to find out, you even named him after your Army buddy. Now think about that. Is it a coincidence that one of your twin sons signed up for the Army while the other was a war resister? I don't think so.

"Unlike me, he was always just like *you*," Richard repeated, each word resounding in the hushed air like the crack of a rifle shot.

Peter reached out his hands toward Richard in wordless supplication. His son glared back at him in stony silence.

"Of course, I was proud of Tommy," said Peter. As soon as Richard heard his father say this, his body went limp. Peter sprang up from the couch and gripped his son by the forearms.

"Hear me out, son! Listen to everything I'm telling you!" he ordered. Jennifer noticed the tone of command in her father-in-law's voice. *That's the voice of the sergeant he was fifty years ago in France.* "You were standing up for your principles, for what you believed in," continued Peter, standing so close to his son their shoulders almost touched. "I was every bit as proud of you for what you did in those days as I was of Tommy."

Richard's eyes widened in astonishment at this revelation.

Jennifer ached to hold her husband tight, but her instincts again warned her not to interfere. She gripped the arm of the couch to keep from getting up and rushing over to him. For several harrowing moments, the incessant din of the crickets overwhelmed her. She felt surrounded, trapped by their constant chatter all around her.

"I never realized you felt that way. About me," said Richard.

"There are things I've never known about you, either," Peter replied gently. "But I'd like to know them. If you'd like to tell me."

"Do you *really* want to know?" asked Richard, his raspy voice conveying both a plea and a challenge.

For years, Peter had wanted his son to ask him such a question. Now, with that moment finally at hand, he was afraid of what he might hear. But even more, he was afraid he never would know if he turned away from whatever the answer might be.

He pursed his lips and, with a slight affirming nod, indicated he would listen to whatever his son chose to tell him.

Richard had always known his father to be a highly reserved and private man who kept his thoughts to himself and expected others to do the same. This was not the response he had expected. He didn't know what to say. His eyes darted about the room as though he were searching for a way out.

Jennifer inched forward on the couch, ready to spring if Richard ran for the door again. But he stood where he was, stock still, his expression gradually becoming one of steely resolve. When he finally spoke, his voice sounded like he had swallowed shards of glass. He coughed to clear his voice.

"April 24, 1970. Remember that day?"

"Of course," moaned Peter. He slumped back down on the couch as if this date had sapped all his remaining strength. But after a few moments, he raised his eyes to his son to let him know he fully intended to listen.

"I was walking across the university quadrangle," said Richard. He spoke slowly . . . precisely, as though each word had to be dragged against its will out of a hiding place deep within his soul. "There was going to be a rally to protest ROTC on campus that afternoon, and I was heading over to it. A friend of mine, Carl Webster, came running up to me and told me that I was to go immediately to the Dean's Office. I thought it might have something to do with the protest and the fact that I was a big deal in SDS."

Detecting the puzzled look on Peter's face, Richard added, "You know—Students for a Democratic Society." Peter indicated he understood, and Richard continued.

"When I got to his office, Dean Matheny had this strange look on his face. At first I thought he was smiling, like he had a joke he wanted to tell me. Why had Dean Matheny called me, of all people, to his office to tell a joke?

"Then I realized it wasn't a smile on his face at all. He looked more like he was going to cry instead. I thought that was pretty weird. All he said was, 'Call home. Now. Use my phone.' Then he hurried out of the room. My hands shook like crazy as I dialed our number. Maybe I already knew. It rang only once."

Peter bent forward and clasped his hands on his lap. He looked to Jennifer like a schoolboy waiting outside the principal's office to be punished. Richard noticed, too. He paused for a moment, long enough for Peter to say, "I answered the phone and said, 'Richie, Tommy is dead. He's been killed in Vietnam.'"

Richard's face screwed up in torment as if he were hearing about his brother's death for the first time. "As soon as I heard you say that, I thought about Tommy and me in that attic, bundled up in our coats, reading your war letters and saluting each other on a snowy winter day, and I thought—"

Richard's thin veneer of calmness cracked. Long-buried grief twisted his face into an anguished mask. He took a deep breath and croaked out the words, "Dad's going to think the wrong twin died."

Trying to get to Richard's side, Peter again pushed himself up off the couch. He wobbled and fell back. Richard took a step toward him, and Jennifer bolted upright. Peter waved them both off to indicate he was alright.

His mind flashed back to when he had been a young father in the 1950s. The present moment faded away, and he saw Tommy and Richard falling off their bikes, skinning their knees on the sidewalk, getting stung by a wasp, coming down with chicken pox. Back then, he had been able to wash and bandage their wounds, put a cold cloth on fevered foreheads, hold them in his arms when they cried.

Peter blinked and returned to the present moment. His son, now a grown man, was standing before him. But on this man's face, Peter recognized the frightened look of the little boy who still needed him. He again pushed himself up from the couch and this time stood up straight and unswerving.

"I would never think such a thing, Richie! Never!" he cried out.

Peter placed his hands over Richard's shoulders. *Is he trying to steady himself or Richard? Or both of them?* wondered Jennifer.

"Never once in my life have I thought that," said Peter emphatically.

Richard wrenched himself free from his father as though he had a contagious disease.

"Don't be too quick to say that," he said, desperately trying to keep control of himself.

Peter shook his head vehemently. "Nothing will ever change how I feel about you." They stared each other in the eye with the intensity of two boxers before the opening bell rings. "Say whatever you need to say, son."

Richard nodded solemnly. "Do you remember the day Tommy left home for Vietnam?" he asked matter-of-factly.

Peter's face scrunched up in pain. "Yes, of course."

"What exactly do you remember?" pressed Richard.

Peter kept his eyes fixed squarely on Richard. "I don't need to tell you about that day," he said. "You were there; you know what happened."

Richard began to protest, but Peter raised his hand to silence him.

"You're right. You deserve an answer to your question," said Peter. He rubbed his hand over his mouth to gain a moment to regain his composure. "That day, when Tommy left to go off to war, I wanted to tell him I loved him. I thought my heart would break wide open if I didn't. But instead, I looked him in the eye, shook his hand, and said, 'Go get 'em!'"

Peter slapped his hand sharply across his forehead. Richard and Jennifer winced simultaneously at the sound.

"What a foolish thing for a father to say to his son! How often have I regretted that moment! He was afraid but determined not to show it. I knew that look. I had seen it in the faces of the boys around me as we headed toward Omaha Beach.

"He gave his mother a long hug and then turned to me. I wanted to hold him like his mother had. Instead he squared his shoulders, extended himself to his full height, and saluted me. I returned his salute, soldier to soldier. He said goodbye, turned, opened the screen door, and walked out like he'd be back in time for supper."

"Before he walked down the porch steps, he clung to the screen door, like it was holding him up. Do you remember?" asked Richard.

"Yes, you're right. I do remember that," replied Peter.

"I was on the porch," said Richard. It sounded to Jennifer like he was talking to himself rather than to them. His eyes were absorbed by a scene only he could see. "I was sitting on the porch swing."

"I seem to remember you boys talking to each other for a few moments," said Peter.

"Did you hear what was said?" Richard asked. Jennifer heard the sudden urgency in his voice and leaned forward, straining to hear every syllable coming out of her husband's mouth.

"No, I was holding onto your mother," said Peter. "She was weeping so hard I could barely make out the sound of your voices. I didn't hear what you said."

"You didn't hear what I said?" asked Richard.

"No, I figured you were saying goodbye to each other. That's all."

Richard turned away from his father.

"What did you say?" asked Jennifer before she could stop herself. Richard glanced over at her. He appeared surprised to see her in the room. She braced for a rebuke. Instead, he bowed his head and sighed like he had been waiting for her to give him the go-ahead before proceeding.

"Just a few words," he said to her and then turned back to his father. His voice took on a dreamlike tone. "Tommy looked at me. He tried to smile but couldn't. He spoke in that squeaky voice he always used to get when he was nervous or scared. He finally managed to say, 'Well, I guess this is it.' He extended his hand to me."

Richard stopped talking. His face flushed crimson. He clenched his fists with such force his knuckles grew white. "I didn't even get up from the swing. Didn't even bother to extend my hand. I looked at him and said—"

Without any warning, Richard bolted for the door. Before Jennifer could react, Peter lunged after him. He grabbed Richard by the arm. Richard struggled halfheartedly for a moment to free himself from his father's grip and then yielded to it.

"What did you say, Richie?" asked Peter, his voice full of compassion and concern.

Richard spoke so softly that Jennifer could hardly hear what he said, "I looked at him and said—"

Peter grasped Richard's shoulder. He gave his son a reassuring squeeze. Richard glanced at him; Peter smiled nervously, trying to encourage him. "It's okay, Richie."

"I looked at him and said, 'My brother, the baby-killer.'"

Peter's legs buckled. Richard clasped his father in his arms to keep him from collapsing to the floor. Jennifer sprang up from the couch. She took a step toward them to help if needed. Richard shook his head to let her know he didn't. He gently lowered Peter down on the couch and took a seat next to him, his arm still around his father's shoulders.

Jennifer went to the sink and poured two glasses of water; then she sat down on the chair by the couch. Each man took one from her and sipped slowly. Richard put his glass down on the coffee table. After a moment, he resumed.

"I couldn't face him. I wanted to take my words back as soon as they were out of my mouth. But in my pride, my foolish, stupid pride, I hesitated. A moment later, I heard the screen door slam. When I looked up, he had disappeared around the corner of the house. I didn't go after him. I don't know why. Maybe it was like you just said. I half expected him to come home in a few hours for supper. Then we'd talk and patch things up, just like we'd always done when we pissed each other off. But I never saw him again. That screen door slamming was the last sound I ever heard him make."

The night before rushed back to Jennifer. *The game of Scrabble . . . the moth . . . the door slamming . . . Richard turning over the board . . . pieces flying across the room . . . Richard running out into the night.*

"Do you still say you don't hate me? For saying that to the son who was just like you?" asked Richard, his voice that of a little boy pleading for reassurance.

Peter went to respond; then he stopped and gazed at Richard's profile. Slowly, he leaned toward his son and kissed him on the temple. Jennifer's body tensed up in anticipation of Richard recoiling from his father's touch. Instead, the son gradually inclined toward his father and rested his head upon his father's shoulder. The wind rustled through the leaves with a lonely, mournful sound.

"Tommy died thinking I hated him," said Richard, his voice breaking. He buried his face in his hands.

Once again, Peter started to reply but hesitated. With his eyes squeezed shut, he shook his head slowly from side to side, as though arguing with a voice only he could hear. "I should have told you a long time ago," he said.

"Told me what?" asked Richard, his face still cradled in his hands and his words muffled.

"There was one more letter added to that bureau drawer," said Peter. "One you never saw."

"From Tommy?" asked Richard.

"Yes," replied Peter after a drawn-out pause.

Jennifer got up from her chair and went to the couch. Despite the pain in her calf, she knelt down before Richard and Peter. She extended a hand to both men, and each held one in both of theirs.

"It wasn't a long letter, not even a full page. He wrote it on his first day in Vietnam. He told us how hot it was, that sort of thing. He hoped he would make me proud of him." Peter's voice broke. For several seconds, he didn't speak.

"At the end of his letter, he said that he would write to us again once he got the time and that he loved all three of us."

Richard looked into Jennifer's eyes. Reassured by her presence next to him, he spoke clearly, his voice strong and steady. "He was killed the next day. On the second day of his tour."

"But he still managed to write that letter," said Peter. "It arrived after we'd learned what had happened to him. Your mother was in so much pain. I couldn't bear to mention his name to tell her. God forgive me, I thought it would be too much for her. So instead, I did what I always did; I stuffed my feelings way down deep along with all the memories of war I couldn't face. As soon as I finished reading that letter, I opened my bureau drawer and shoved it underneath all the other letters. All the way in the back. Then I slammed the drawer shut."

Richard turned his body and bent his head slightly toward his father. Peter could only glance at him before averting his eyes. He opened his mouth to speak, but no words came out. *What else is he afraid of?* thought Jennifer.

"There was—one more thing," said Peter, but he couldn't bring himself to continue.

"Tell us when you're ready, Pop," said Jennifer tenderly.

After a few seconds, he turned to gaze for a moment at her, then at Richard, and then straight ahead at the last flickering cinder on the hearth.

"The letter had a postscript. It said, 'Tell Richie I love him. Nothing will ever change that. I'll write to him next. I know he didn't mean what he said.'"

Peter turned to his son with a faraway look in his eyes. "I never understood what he meant by that. Now I do."

Peter slowly took his hand away from Jennifer's hold and rested his chin in his palms as though trying to hold his head up. "I closed that dresser drawer and never opened it again," he said, his voice barely a whisper. "I forced everything it contained out of my mind. At least, at the time, that's what I thought I did. But I guess my mind doesn't work that way."

Peter put his hand on Richard's shoulder.

"What a damn fool I've been. You've suffered all these years because you didn't know the truth," said Peter, his words clear and forceful until they faltered with emotion. "And it's all my fault."

"No, Dad. You're not a fool. And it's not your fault. If I hadn't said what I did that day on the porch—" began Richard. "I never had the chance to tell him I'm sorry. But I am. I'm sorry. I'm so sorry." He buried his face against his father's shoulder.

Jennifer wrapped her arms around both men and held them tightly.

CHAPTER EIGHTEEN
Another Train in the Afternoon

THE NEXT DAY DAWNED overcast. The sky threatened rain any moment, but not a drop fell. When the first rays of sun broke through the clouds, the lake reflected the cerulean-blue sky.

Peter awakened first. It had been his habit since his days in the Army to get out of bed immediately upon awakening. This morning, however, he propped up his pillow so he had a partial view of the lake. Something about the way the sunlight glistened on the water filled him with a vague longing he was not able to identify.

Up until yesterday, he had dismissed all such nebulous feelings as not being worth the time it took to consider them. Now, as he lay in bed, it pained him to realize he had no idea what his heart was trying to tell him. He promised himself he would practice listening—not just to others, but to himself as well.

He heard either Jennifer or Richard walking around in the kitchen. Throwing back the blanket and top sheet, he sprang out of bed. As he did every morning, he stretched toward the ceiling and touched his toes a dozen times. He made the bed with hospital corners and stretched the sheets and blanket tight enough to bounce a quarter. The delicious fragrance of something made with apple-cinnamon baking in the oven made his mouth water. So did the aroma of percolating freshly ground coffee.

He showered, dressed, and packed his suitcase. When he finished, he glanced around the room to make sure he was leaving everything exactly as he had found it. He checked the departure time on his train ticket. It was scheduled to leave the station at 10:00 AM. He had just the right amount of time to get there without rushing. Placing the ticket on the bed beside the suitcase, Peter opened the door and walked into the kitchen.

Jennifer and Richard were sitting at the table, sipping cups of coffee. Freshly baked apple-cinnamon muffins were in a wicker basket at the center of the table. Next to the basket was a cut-glass bowl of blueberries, sliced strawberries, honeydew melons, and bananas. Another bowl just like the first contained vanilla yogurt. Peter saw there was a coffee cup inside a bowl on top of a plate at his place. He was touched that Jennifer had gone to so much trouble.

Richard rose from his chair as soon as Peter walked into the room. He went to the stove, brought the coffeepot to the table, picked up his father's cup, and poured coffee into it.

Peter thanked him as he sat down. Richard nodded and brought the coffeepot back to the stove.

"If I remember correctly, you like your coffee black in the morning," said Richard as he sat back down at the table.

"Yes, that's right," replied Peter, taking a cautious sip of the steaming brew.

"I was going to say, we have cream and sugar if your tastes have changed," Richard offered, a little too eagerly, inadvertently revealing the anxiety he was trying to conceal. Peter held up his hand to decline the offer as he took another sip. He spooned some of the fruit and yogurt, and then he mixed fruit into his bowl. Richard and Jennifer waited for him to finish and then did the same.

"Looks like it will be a nice day after all," observed Richard as Peter sipped his coffee. Richard continued, "I wasn't sure what to expect when I first looked out the window." He paused, searching for words to finish his thought. "I think it's going to be a nice day."

Peter nodded. Jennifer noticed how each held the mug with the handle facing out and blew across the surface of the coffee before taking a sip. "Yes, it looked like rain for a while there," he replied. He was about to say the coffee was the best he had tasted in a very long time but decided not to say anything that might be mistaken for mere flattery, even though it happened to be true.

For what felt like a long, drawn-out minute—but was really only a matter of seconds—nobody spoke. The only sounds were spoons clinking against bowls until Richard asked somewhat abruptly, "What time is your train leaving today?"

Peter was just raising another spoonful of fruit and yogurt to his mouth. He froze, the spoon hovering between his mouth and the bowl. Richard realized at once, without even seeing the pained look in his father's eyes, that his words had stung.

"No! No!" he rushed to explain. "That's not what I meant." Peter's eyes remained downcast, fixed blankly on his bowl of fruit and yogurt.

Richard peered at Jennifer, not sure what to do. "Go ahead— tell him your idea," she whispered encouragingly.

His mouth set tight in an anxious grimace, he looked back at his father. "What I meant to say was—"

He faltered and fell silent. Jennifer took hold of his hand.

"What I meant was," repeated Richard, steadied by his wife's touch, "there are those chrysanthemums on the porch. You know, the ones for that unknown soldier you told us about?"

It took a second for Peter to realize what his son was talking about. His hurt expression gave way to one of confusion. "Oh," he said, not sure what Richard's point was. "I guess I forgot all about them."

Peter glanced at Jennifer and shrugged his shoulders. "Well, it was a nice thought anyhow," he said.

"I think there's still time to get them planted," Richard said apprehensively.

"No, my train leaves in less than two hours," replied Peter. "I'd be cutting it too close."

"There's another train in the afternoon," said Richard. "One at four o'clock. Is that right?" he asked Jennifer, though he knew the time because he had already checked the departure schedule several times while lying in bed. She winked her confirmation.

Peter searched Richard's face, still not entirely sure he understood what his son was saying.

"I'd like to help you plant the chrysanthemums," declared Richard. "If that would be okay with you, of course."

Peter tried coming across as nonchalant, afraid too much enthusiasm might somehow scare his son off. "Yes, that would be okay with me," he replied as casually as he could.

They continued eating in silence. But unlike other times in the past two days, it was the kind of peaceful silence that spreads over the lake just as the sun comes through the pine trees ringing the eastern hills.

After they finished, all three rose from the table. Richard went outside and pulled the wheelbarrow and two shovels out from the small shed in back of the cottage. He filled the watering can to the top and placed it in the wheelbarrow. Peter then put in the flowers, and Richard picked up the handles. When they were ready to go, both men looked up at Jennifer, observing them as she stood on the porch.

"Coming along?" Richard asked.

She shook her head. "You two go ahead," she told them with a little catch in her throat.

Richard nodded, and Peter gave her a little wave.

Jennifer watched them as they walked along, side by side. She wasn't able to make out what Peter said to Richard that caused them both to laugh as they came to the bend in the path leading to the grave of an unknown soldier.

The End

Made in the USA
Lexington, KY
24 November 2019

57607694R00112